THE HEALTHY

Dead

THE
HEALTHY
Dead

A Tale of Bauchelain and Korbal Broach

Steven Erikson

Introduction by Paul Kearney

PS Publishing 2004

FIRST EDITION

Published in May 2004 by PS Publishing LLP
by arrangement with the author.
All rights reserved by the author.

ISBN
1 904619 08 8 (Paperback)
1 904619 09 6 (Hardcover)

PS Publishing LLP
Hamilton House
4 Park Avenue
Harrogate HG2 9BQ
ENGLAND

e-mail
editor@pspublishing.co.uk

Internet
http://www.pspublishing.co.uk

Introduction

By Paul Kearney

Fantasy—now, how would one define it? There's a lot of it out there, it must be said, hecatombs of high-falutin tales sprung from the fevered imaginations of a fervent band of devotees. Some might think it's an easy genre to master. Up springs a callow youth of uncertain heritage, his childhood leavened with the usual omens and uncanny coincidences, and then lo and behold, he discovers a yen to wander, to take a look at the wide world the author has made up around him. Throw in a sidekick, a magic sword, and preferably a dragon or two, *et voila*. Simplicity itself.

There's a lot of it out there, as I said, and there are those who think that the rules of the genre are inescapable. This chap you're about to read though, this Erikson fellow; he drives a freight train through the rules. He leaves you wiping dust out of your eyes and wondering what the hell just went by.

Wizards, sure. Warriors by the thousand. Assassins, nobles, beggars, eccentrics, gods, demons. We've seen them all before—but not done like this. The world of the Malazan Empire is jaw-droppingly complex, and the folk who inhabit it no less so. It may seem a deceptively obvious thing to say, but they are *real* people, whose motives are mixed, whose souls are contorted by the travails of their everyday lives. I like that—I always have. To take fantasy and make it as *real* as possible - in this genre that is the sign of real artistry.

A handful of examples, out of the teeming multitudes. firstly, Erikson's Magic. It is the most complex, believable, (if that's the right term) and *visceral* system of magic I've ever encountered, in any book, anywhere. It *feels* right. It also feels incredibly dangerous.

His fighting men—they are soldiers. They speak as soldiers should. They are not heroes, but men of work, professionals. Their calling makes them tired and old and sets a canker at their heart.

His primitive peoples—and here I will confess to sheer, unadulterated envy at his knowledge and the use of it—are authentic down to the dirt beneath their nails. Erikson knows how these civilizations operate at a basic level, how it feels to kindle fire in a wilderness, and listen to the night-noises whilst the stars blaze overhead. It is a knowledge that cannot be assumed, but must be integral to the writer's psyche.

The story which follows is lighter in tone than most of the material which concerns the Malazan Empire, its rise and fall, but the invention and sheer panache on display are no less impressive. It is a tale which begs to be read out loud amid a crowd of like-minded folk in a firelit pub, preferably with clouds of pipe-smoke winding through the air (and no doubt some would-be Well Knights looking on in disapproval.) The wealth of the ideas within are staggering, but they troop on stage in so modest and winsome a fashion that it is easy to pass them by, to take for granted the ingenuity and sheer originality of their crafting. Reading Erikson, one begins by thinking that he has started a hare for the hell of it, just because he's been distracted by an idea, a concept, a character. After a while there are a litter of these things up and running, all bright-eyed and full of beans, but by the end of the story he has them all in the bag again—he's brought them to the end he had in mind at the beginning. He makes it look easy, and it's anything but.

To put it another, more personal way—and speaking as a writer—again and again upon reading Erikson I find myself grinding my teeth, slapping my forehead and groaning; *'Damn! I wish I'd thought of that!'* In such an egocentric profession as this, there can be no higher praise.

Paul Kearney
February 2004

Warning to lifestyle fascists everywhere.
Don't read this or you'll go blind.

'Those who die healthily are stuffed and displayed
in glass-cased shrines as examples of good living'

*I*MID FACTALLO, foreman of the work crew re-laying the
cobbles round back of the Wall, was struck unconscious by a
collapsing wagon, and so became a saint. His fellow workers, their
faces smeared in dust, stared down upon him in wonder as he
blinked open his eyes. The sky behind those mundane visages
looked indeed the resplendent residence of the Lady of Beneficence, the Goddess of Wellness, into whose finely-boned arms
Imid Factallo felt himself on the verge of falling. If, of course, one
could indeed fall upward, plunging clear of the heavy, laden earth,
and dive with keening joy into the vast blueness overhead.

But the glorious ascent never arrived. Instead, runners had
set out to the Grand Temple and were now returning, this time
leading worthies, their pink shirts and pantaloons bound at the
joints, arms and legs filled out with padding to infer to any and all
onlookers the musculature of vigorous health, their drawn faces
painted in flushed tones. And joining them, three Well Knights,
white-cloaked and clanking in the highly polished, silver-etched
armour of their exalted rank—and Imid saw, foremost among
these three, none other than Invett Loath, Purest of the Paladins,
who needed no rouge to colour his square-jawed, large-nosed
face, which was very nearly purple, so thoroughly blooded the
veins and arteries beneath the only-so-slightly spotty skin. Imid
knew as well as any other citizen that one might, upon seeing
Knight Invett Loath for the first time, assume the very worst—

that the Paladin was far too fond of ale, wine and the other forbidden vices of slovenly living—but this was not the case. Invett Loath could not be pre-eminent among the Knights were he such a fallen soul. In fact, nothing untoward had passed his lips his entire life. At least inward.

"You, sir," he now rumbled, glaring down from beneath the rim of his blindingly sunlit helm, "are the unworthy leach of the salt marshes they call Imid Factallo? Has your skull cracked entirely open, then? Are you now mute as well as dumb? The Goddess abides both the physically and the mentally inept, you will be pleased to know, sir. Thus leaving you twice, if not thrice blessed. It is a distinction to ponder, is it not? Yet I see your eyes dart, suggesting that sight has not left you. Twice, then, as I first surmised. Well, Imid Factallo, once foreman of the Wall's Third Reach road-tossers, you will now be honoured to know that, by your fated accident which has spilled your blood so messily onto your face and the stones beneath you, I now pronounce you a Saint of the Lady."

Imid Factallo stared up at the Knight, then, squeezing shut his eyes, he groaned and wished, with all his heart, that the damned wagon had killed him.

"THE TRADER CALLED the city Quaint," Emancipor Reese said, squinting at the distant high walls with their strange banners dangling limp two-thirds of the way up. The battered wagon beneath the two men pitched wildly on the rocky path.

"Well," Bauchelain sighed beside him, "there is little I see to support that observation."

"No, Master, it is actually called *Quaint*, the last and most remote of the city-states on this peninsula. And, given that we've seen naught of even so much as a hamlet in the past six days, I would agree with the trader that it is indeed remote."

"Perhaps," the sorceror conceded, pulling at his pointed beard. "Nonetheless, the only quality I can discern from this distance that might be construed as quaint, is that tidy row of corpses spiked to the inland wall."

Emancipor narrowed his gaze even further. Not banners, then, dangling so limp. "And you call that quaint, Master?"

"Yes, I do, Mister Reese. Korbal Broach will be pleased, don't you think?"

The manservant leaned back on the wagon's buckboard, easing the knots in his lower back. "I would hazard, Master," he offered, "that the city's authorities would not look kindly upon the theft of their... uh, decorations."

"I imagine you are correct," Bauchelain murmured, his high brow wrinkling in thought. "More alarming, perhaps, is the notion that our recent escapades in the previous city might have preceded our mortal selves."

Emancipor Reese shivered and clutched tighter the traces in his gnarled hands. "I sincerely hope otherwise, Master."

"Perhaps, this time, we ought not to risk it. What do you say, Mister Reese? Circumvent the city. Find ourselves an outlying village and purchase a worthy sea craft, and so make our way across the bay?"

"Excellent idea, Master."

The road had been empty of passersby during the course of their conversation, and the dust trailing the wake of the trader who had been heading the other way was already settling on the tree-tops visible beyond the road's crumbly edge. As if to challenge Bauchelain's decision, however, there came the sound of boots scrabbling up the track towards them, and a moment later two figures climbed into view. A man and a woman, carrying between them a small but clearly heavy chest.

IN THIS WORLD of virtues, the third and most reviled demon, Vice, knew loneliness, despair and misery. Which wasn't right, all things considered. Of the three emotional states previously mentioned, Ineb Cough was well-acquainted with the latter two. Despair and misery, but they were what he delivered unto others. To suffer beneath identical torment as those who succumbed to his lures was unconscionable. Well, perhaps that was the wrong word to use, but the sentiment fit.

Which was more than could be said of the foppish dancer's clothes he was presently wearing, clothes that clearly had belonged to a much taller, wider-shouldered individual. It was a sad truth, he reflected as he poked through the rubbish in the alley behind The Palace of Earthy Delights looking for... something, anything. A sad truth, that the arts of the flesh could not but surrender to decrepitude, eventually. That talent and prowess gave way to aching muscles and brittle bones. The world had no place for aged artists, and that brutal fact could not have been made more evident than with the demon's discovery of the dead dancer. His wrinkled face staring sightless up at the sky, the expression revealing faint surprise, perhaps even outrage, to announce the final realisation that, bent and old as he'd become, he could no longer perform that particular move. That, indeed, the loud crack that had no doubt accompanied that final spin and twirl was unquestionably a bad thing.

The demon doubted that there had been an audience. Another sordid fact of aged artists—no one watched, no one cared. Spin, twirl, snap, sprawling onto the grubby cobblestones, there to lie undisturbed by any but the tiny eaters of the flesh that dwelt within a living body and would only now come out to feed.

Vice had always been the retreat of artists. When naught else remained, there was always drink. Dubious carnal appetites. An excess of indulgences served on overflowing plates. The host of delectable death-wishes to sample among the myriad substances that were offered. Or, had been offered. Back in the good old days.

But now, in Quaint, virtues ruled, righteous and supreme. And people danced in the streets. Well, some people did, or tried to, only to die trying. Likely a final flourish. There were plenty of those these days. To live clean, to live with unobstructed vigour. To die slow. To die sudden. But always to die, alas. The demon, who might well have wished to die, could not. He persisted, in the manner of hidden desires, and so was witness to the unchanging realities of these sad mortals. Ducking and dodging the inevitable awakening of those tiny eaters of flesh. In the end . . . was the end, and only the end. Poor sods.

How many pleasures, Ineb wondered morosely, were truly pristine? How many lives swanned past the multitude of ambushes the physical world set in their path? This was another kind of dance, with frantically flapping wings on the heels, and it was a style singularly unattractive. Strident, precious, defensive in gesture, spasmodic in extremity. The demon found it depressing to witness. After all, what *didn't* kill?

Amidst the rubbish behind the Palace of Earthy Delights, his rummaging hands touched and closed on an object. A large bottle of fired clay, the base chipped and the neck broken off, but otherwise . . . perfect. The demon drew it into view. Yes, it had once held liquor.

Ineb could not help the broadening smile that split his pocked, grubby face, as he lifted the bottle to his nose and breathed deep its stale aroma. Years old, likely, back when the Palace had been an altogether different kind of establishment, when within its confines something other than green leaves had been on offer.

His flabby lips reached out to caress the cold glaze, to nibble at the smooth pattern of the maker's seal. Red-tipped tongue flitted out along the neck's sharp edge. He sniffed, snorted, stroked with his fingers, and crouched down in the rubbish. Just as there were tiny eaters of flesh, so too were there tiny, unseen creatures that clung to the memories of flavour, of smell. It would take him half the night before the bottle yielded the last morsel.

"*H*AVE YOU EVER wondered, what happened to Lust?"

Nauseo Sloven's miniscule eyes thinned amidst the flaccid folds of fat, but the only reply he made was a loud, bilious exudence of gas from somewhere below. He reached out one oily, smeared hand and plucked up a fat grub from the heap of rotting vegetables, and carefully set it down on his protruding tongue, which then snapped inward. A brief crunch, then a smack of lips.

"You'd think," Senker Later continued, stifling a yawn, "that of us all, she'd be the most . . . persistent."

"Maybe," Nauseo wheezed, "that is why we never see her." He waved a hand about. "This alley evinces our poor lot these days, abandoned as it is to underfed rats, squealing maggots, and diffident memories of past glory. Not to mention our pathetic brother, Ineb Cough."

"Your memories, not mine," Senker Later said, wrinkling her small, button nose. "Your glories existed in excess, all of which was far too frantic for my tastes. No, this alley and its modest pace suits me just fine." She stretched her less than clean bared legs out and settled deeper amidst the rubbish. "I see no reason to leave, and even less to complain."

"I applaud your consistency," Nauseo said, "and your aplomb, even as you lie here night after night witnessing my diminishment. Look at me. I am nothing but folds of skin. Even the smell about my person has gone from foul to musty to earthy, as if I was no more than a rotting tree stump in some sunlit glade. And, might I point out with apologies for my seeming indelicacy, you are far less than you once were, my dear. Who has succumbed to your charms of late?"

"No one. But I admit I can't be bothered to worry much about it."

"And so you will while away into extinction, Senker Later."

She sighed. "I suppose you're right. Something should be done."

"Such as?"

"Oh, I'll think about it later. Look, there's a nice fat grub, crawling out—there!"

"I see it. Too far away, alas."

Senker Later smiled at him sweetly. "That was nice, thank you."

THE CHEST WAS filled with coins. Sunset gold and piss-bleached silver, a glitter of poison to Emancipor Reese's jaded eyes. Nothing good ever came of riches, nothing, nothing at all.

"We're Saints of Glorious Labour," the one named Imid Factallo said.

"This seems a worthy title," Bauchelain observed as he stood before the two Quaint citizens with hands clasped behind his back.

Nearby, Emancipor had started a small cook fire and was now preparing mulled wine against the growing chill. Modest, mundane tasks had a way of accompanying egregious, enormous evils. It had always been so, he believed. Especially in the company of his masters. And he sensed that something truly ignoble was in the offing.

"A worthy title, you say," Imid replied, looking like he had just swallowed a mouthful of ashes. "So you'd think!"

"So I do," Bauchelain replied, brows lifting, "and have just stated it."

"Well, it's a misery, I tell you," Imid said, a twitch rippling along his left cheek. "I'm out of work. Now I spend all day praying with a thousand other saints. Saints! The only thing we all have in common is clumsy stupidity or rotten luck, or both."

"You are too harsh on yourself, sir," Bauchelain said. "To have earned such a noble title—"

"One must nearly die whilst working," the woman cut in, her voice harsh. "Mistakes, accidents, blind chance—these are what makes saints in Quaint!"

Bauchelain had frowned at the interruption, and now the frown deepened. He drew his long, silk-lined cloak tighter about himself. "If I am to understand you, the proclamation of saint-hood depends upon injuries sustained in public service?"

"You have it precisely," Imid Factallo said. "Let me explain about Quaint. It all began with the sudden death of the previous king, Necrotus the Nihile. Your usual kind of ruler. Petty, vicious and corrupt. We liked him just fine. But then he died and his little known brother assumed the throne. And that's when everything started to unravel."

The woman beside Imid said, "King Macrotus, the Overwhelmingly Considerate, and there's no love in that title."

"And your name is?"

"Saint Elas Sil, sir. I had a fellow worker trip into me with a knitting needle. Stabbed me in the neck, the idiot. I bled all over the wool, and it turns out that's a debt even being a saint doesn't forgive. Only, how can I make restitution? I'm not permitted to work!"

"A newly invoked law by your new king, then."

Emancipor stirred the mulling wine. The smell was making him light-headed in a pleasant, dreamy manner. He leaned back on his haunches and began stoking his clay pipe with rustleaf and durhang. His actions had snared the attentions of the two saints, and Emancipor saw Elas lick her lips.

"It is the Will of Wellness," Imid Factallo said, nodding up at Bauchelain. "Macrotus has elevated the cult of the Lady of Beneficence. It now stands as the city's official—and only legal—religion."

Emancipor narrowed his gaze as he met the woman's eyes. She would have been attractive, he mused, had she been born someone else. As it was, Elas Sil, the saint with the puckered neck, might or might not have been the victim of an accident. The servant set burning ember to his pipe. He recalled, vaguely, that some old hag in his home city of Lamentable Moll had lived by similar notions of wellness. Perhaps the trend was spreading, like some kind of horrific plague.

Imid Factallo continued, "The new Prohibitions are filling volumes. The list of That Which Kills grows daily and the healers are frantically searching for yet more."

"And all that kills," Elas Sil said, "is forbidden. The king wants his people to be healthy, and since most people won't do what's necessary for themselves, Macrotus will do it on their behalf."

"If you want the Lady's Blessings in the afterlife," Imid said, "then die healthily."

"Die *un*healthily," Elas said, "and there's no burial. Your corpse is hung upside-down on the outer wall."

"Well," Bauchelain said, "how is it that we may help you? Clearly, you cannot be unmade saints. Nor, as you see, are we simple travelers in possession of an army."

Though there's one chasing us. But Emancipor kept that addendum to himself.

Imid Factallo and Elas Sil exchanged looks, then the former ducked his head and leaned slightly forward. "It's not the traders' season, but word travels anyway. Fishing boats and such." He tapped his misshapen nose. "I got a friend with a good sight on this road, starting at the top of Hurba's Hill, so word came in plenty of time."

"You're the ones," Elas Sil said in a low voice, her eyes still fixed on Emancipor as he stirred the wine. A flicker towards Bauchelain. "Two, but three in all. Half of the last city you visited is nothing but ashes—"

"A misunderstanding, I assure you," Bauchelain murmured.

Imid Factallo snorted. "That ain't what we heard—"

Bauchelain cleared his throat, his warning frown silencing the saint. "One must presume, therefore, that even as you anticipated our salubrious arrival, so too has your king. Accordingly, it is unlikely he would welcome our presence."

"Macrotus cares little for tales from neighbouring cities— they're all cess-pits of depravity, after all."

"And his advisors and military commanders are equally ignorant? What of his court mages?"

"They're all gone, the mages. Banished. As for the rest," Imid shrugged, "such interest would be direly viewed by Macrotus, hinting as it would of unpleasant appetites, or at least dangerous curiosity."

"The wine is ready," Emancipor announced.

The heads of the two saints snapped round with avid, hungry stares.

Elas Sil whispered, "We are forbidden all such ... vices."

The manservant's brows rose. "Absolute abstinence?"

"Weren't you listening?" Imid growled. "All illegal in Quaint. No alcohol, no rustleaf, no durhang, no dream-powders. Not for saints, not for anyone."

Elas Sil added, "No meat, only vegetables and fruit and three-finned fish. Butchery is cruel and red meat is unhealthy besides."

"No whoring, no gambling," Imid said. "All such pleasures are suspect."

Emancipor grunted in reply to all of that. He tapped his pipe against his heel and spat a throatful of phlegm onto the fire.

"Curious," Bauchelain said. "What is it you wish us to do for you?"

"Usurp the king," Imid Factallo said.

"Usurp, as in depose."

"Right."

"Depose, as in remove."

"Yes."

"Remove, as in kill."

The saints looked at one another again. But neither replied.

Bauchelain turned to study the distant city. "I am inclined," he said, "to preface my acceptance of your offer with a warning—

a last opportunity, if you will, to say not another word, to simply collect your coins and return home—and I and my entourage will blithely move on to some other city. This warning, then. In this world, there are worse things than a considerate king."

"That's what you think," said Elas Sil.

Bauchelain offered her a benign smile.

"That's it?" Imid Factallo demanded. "No more questions?"

"Oh, many more questions, my good sir," Bauchelain replied. "Alas, you are not the ones to whom I would ask them. You may go."

WELL KNIGHT INVETT LOATH stood above the basket with the wailing baby and glared at the half-dozen women talking near the well. "Whose child is this?"

One woman separated herself from the group and hurried over. "It's colic, Oh Gloriously Pure One. Nothing to be done for it, alas."

The Well Knight's face reddened. "Absurd," he snapped. "There must be some sort of treatment to silence this whelp. Have you not heard the most recent Prohibition? Loud babies are to be confiscated for disturbing the well-being of citizens. They are to be delivered to the Temple of the Lady, where they will be taught the Ways of Beneficence, said ways including vows of silence."

The hapless mother had gone pale at Invett's words. The other women at the well were quickly collecting their children and hastening away. "But," she stammered, "the medicines we used to use are now illegal—"

"Medicines made illegal? Are you mad?"

"They contained forbidden substances. Alcohol. Dur-hang—"

"You mothers were in the habit of befouling the blood and spirit of your children?" The notion made Invett apoplectic. "Is it any wonder such gross abuse was forbidden? And you dare call yourself a loving mother?"

She picked up the basket. "I didn't know! I'll take her home—"

"Too late for that." He gestured and the three worthies standing behind him rushed forward. They struggled with the woman for control of the basket, until one of the worthies poked the mother in the eye. She yelped and staggered back, releasing her grip on the basket, and the worthies hurried off with it down the street. The woman wailed beseechingly.

"Silence!" Invett bellowed. "Public displays of emotion are forbidden! You risk arrest!"

She fell to her knees and began pleading in a most unseemly manner.

"Clean yourself up, woman," Invett said, lip curling, "and be glad for my mercy."

He marched off, in the wake of his worthies with their shrieking charge.

Before long they arrived at the Grand Temple of the Lady. The formal front entrance with its raised platform and the blockish altar sitting atop it—from which the Lady's voice periodically emerged to deliver her pronouncements—had been deemed too public for the delivery of wailing babes. Accordingly, Invett and his worthies approached a side postern where one worthy knocked in elaborate rhythm. A moment's wait, then the door creaked open.

"Give me that," Invett said, taking the basket with its blubbering, red-faced infant. He stepped into the corridor beyond and closed the door behind him.

The priestess facing him, veiled and robed but not so disguised as to hide her near obesity, was staring down at the babe with hungry eyes. "Most excellent," she whispered. "The third today. The Lady is delighted with this new Prohibition."

"I'm surprised," Invett growled. "Soon you will have a thousand screaming babes in here, and how will the Lady know peace?"

The priestess reached out and pinched the soft part of the baby's nearest arm. "Plump," she murmured. "Good, yes. The Temple's peace will not suffer for long."

Invett Loath frowned, wondering what it was in her words that made him slightly uneasy, then with a grunt he dismissed it. Not for the Well Knight to question other servants to the Lady. He handed her the basket.

The baby, that had been screaming all this time, all at once fell silent.

Knight and priestess leaned forward, studied its suddenly wide eyes.

"Like a newborn sparrow," the priestess murmured, "when a jay is near."

"I know nothing of birds," Invett Loath said. "I am leaving now."

"Yes, you are."

A CROW PERCHED on the buckboard of the wagon, feathers ruffling in the breeze that had sprung up as the sun's light faded. Emancipor noted its arrival with a scowl. "Is he hungry, do you think?"

Bauchelain, who was seated on a folding camp stool opposite his manservant, gave a single shake of his head. "He has fed."

"Why are you looking at me like that, Master?"

"I have been thinking, Mister Reese."

Oh no. "About deposing this kindly king?"

"Kindly? Do you not realise, Mister Reese, how perfectly diabolical is this king's genius? Every tyranny imaginable is possible when prefaced by the notion that it is for the well being of the populace. Patronising? Of course, but when delivered with wide-eyed innocence and earnestness, what is a citizen to do? Complain about the benefits? Hardly, not when guilt is the benign torturer's first weapon of choice. No," Bauchelain rose to his feet and turned to face the dark city. He used both hands to sweep his hair back, his eyes glittering in the gloom, "we are witness to genius, plain and simple. And now, we are about to match wits with this clever king. I admit, the blood rushes about my being at the challenge."

"I am happy for you, Master."

"Ah, Mister Reese, I gather you still do not understand the threat this king poses to such creatures as you and I."

"Well, frankly, no, I don't, Master. As you say."

"I must perforce make the linkage plain, of sufficient simplicity to permit your uneducated mind to grasp all manner of significance. Desire for goodness, Mister Reese, leads to earnestness. Earnestness in turn leads to sanctimonious self-righteousness, which breeds intolerance, upon which harsh judgment quickly follows, yielding dire punishment, inflicting general terror and paranoia, eventually culminating in revolt, leading to chaos, then dissolution, and thus, the end of civilisation." He slowly turned, looked down upon Emancipor. "And we are creatures dependent upon civilisation. It is the only environment in which we can thrive."

Emancipor frowned. "The desire for goodness leads to the end of civilisation?"

"Precisely, Mister Reese."

"But if the principal aim is to achieve good living and health among the populace, what is the harm in that?"

Bauchelain sighed. "Very well, I shall try again. Good living and health, as you say, yielding well being. But well being is a contextual notion, a relative notion. Perceived benefits are measured by way of contrast. In any case, the result is smugness, and from that an overwhelming desire to deliver conformity among those perceived as less pure, less fortunate—the unenlightened, if you will. But conformity leads to ennui, and then indifference. From indifference, Mister Reese, dissolution follows as a natural course, and with it, once again, the end of civilisation."

"All right all right, Master, we are faced with the noble task of confounding the end of civilisation."

"Well said, Mister Reese. I admit I find the ethical aspects of our mission surprisingly... refreshing."

"Have you a plan, then?"

"Indeed. And yes, you will be required to play an essential role."

"Me?"

"You must enter the city, Mister Reese. Unobtrusively, of course. Once there, you must complete the following missions...."

*T*HE SIGHTLESS EYES had been staring a long time without seeing anything. Not surprising, since ravens had long since eaten everything there was to eat within those hoary sockets. No lids left with which to blink, nor any fluids to bring tears to those withered rims. Even so, Necrotus the Nihile, once king of Quaint, was not entirely surprised to find a grainy, misshapen scene slowly form, spreading to fill the vista his soul faced, a vista that had heretofore been naught but darkness—the welcome that was the Abyss.

Being dragged back and made to inhabit this bird-picked desiccated corpse hanging on the city's north wall, the flesh he had once called his own in better days, was, while not surprising, nonetheless disappointing. Worse yet, he found he could talk. "Who has done this to me?"

A voice answered from somewhere below, not far, perhaps level with his chest. "To that, I have more than one answer, King Necrotus."

The tether upon which his soul was bound to this body was not so tight as to prevent a slight wandering outward, in order to look down. So that he could see the two crows perched upon the rusty spike projecting out from the wall, upon which his corpse had been impaled. "Ah," Necrotus said, "now I understand."

One of the crows cocked its head. "You do? How charming."

"Yes. You have come to discuss me. My life. My fate, all the lost loves of my mortal years in this world. Only, why must I witness this ironic indulgence?"

"Actually," the first crow said, "we would discuss, not you, but your brother."

"Macrotus? That sniveling worm? Why?"

"For one, he is now king."

"Oh. Of course. I should have thought of that. No heirs. Well, plenty of bastards, but the laws are strict on that. I was planning on officially adopting one, but then he died. And before I could choose another, so did I."

"Indeed. That strikes me as careless," the first crow said. "In any case, my companion has done some cursory examination of your corpse here, and has detected the remnants of poison."

Necrotus thought about that. "That runt did me in! Gods below, I never thought he had it in him!"

"More precisely," the crow continued, "he fouled your life-extending alchemies, Necrotus. Which strikes us as odd, given his eagerness for health."

"I was cheating, though, wasn't I? He hated that. He invented a mechanism, you know. Fills an entire room. He climbs into a harness and it works all his muscles, all his joints, it exercises him, jerks him about. He spends half his day in that thing. I concluded he'd gone insane."

"Tell us," the crow said, "of this Lady of Beneficence."

"A goddess, a minor one. Severe, miserable, a nose like a pig's, tilted up, you understand. At least it's so on the statues and idols depicting her."

"A goddess?"

"I assume so. Believed to dwell in a pit in the Grand Temple. Why?"

"She is now the city's official patroness."

"That bloodthirsty bitch? Gods below! If I wasn't a shriveled up thing hanging here, I'd—I'd—well, it'd be different!"

"Well, King Necrotus, I would point out, you are not alone here on these walls."

"I'm not?"

"And so I now ask you, are you of a mind to partake in ousting your brother, the King of Quaint?"

"Beats hanging around. Let's hear your plan, corbies."

EMANCIPOR STOOD in front of the small bush, listening to the birds chirp to greet the morning whilst he emptied his bladder.

"Look well on that yellow, murky stream, Mister Reese—"

The manservant started at the voice beside him. "Master! You, uh, surprised me."

"Thus reducing you to a trickle. I believe, in case you are interested, that only a few minor cantrips would convert the toxins in your flow, such that a single gesture could set that unfortunate shrub to flame. But as I said, look well, Mister Reese. In a few days you will be astonished to witness a stream issuing from you so clear that it is nigh water."

Emancipor finished with a few final, spasmodic spurts, gave himself a shake, tucked in, then fumbled at retying the front of his trousers. "I'm afraid I don't understand you, Master—"

"To dwell unobtrusively in the city, Mister Reese, you shall have to abstain from all unhealthy indulgences. You might well return from this mission a new man."

The manservant stared at Bauchelain. "Abstain? Completely? But, can't I sneak anything—"

"Absolutely not, Mister Reese. Now, divest yourself of the relevant items on your person. The crowd of traders on the low road is reaching ideal density."

"I'm not sure I want to do this."

"Ah, but you are in my employ, are you not? Our contract stipulates—"

"All right! Of course, Master," he added. In a calmer tone, "Can I not break my fast, as it were, before heading down there?"

"Oh, very well. Let it not be said I am a cruel master."

They returned to the encampment, where Reese quickly filled his pipe with rustleaf and durhang, and broke the wax-sealed stopper on a bottle of wine.

"When you are done," Bauchelain said, standing nearby and watching, "there is some wild anise growing here beside the trail. Chew the feathery leaves. This should assist in hiding the various smells emanating from your person. Would that we could find some wild garlic, onions, skunk-bulbs .... Not too much of that wine, Mister Reese, it will not do to have you weaving and staggering at Quaint's gates. You are producing enough smoke to launch a fire-fighting crew from the city—I think that will be enough, Mister Reese. The anise—"

"It's fennel, Master," Emancipor said.

"It is? Well, whatever."

Head buzzing, the manservant marched over to the weeds and began pulling the thin spidery leaves from the stalks. "I feel like a damned caterpillar."

"The white and black banded ones?" Bauchelain asked. "I am pleased to inform you that those transform into the most beautiful butterflies."

Emancipor stared over at his master.

Who stared back.

A moment of silence, then Bauchelain cleared his throat. "Yes, well, off you go, then."

IMID FACTALLO WANDERED down Runner's Avenue, strange twitches spasming across half his face. They had started up a few days ago, some consequence of the wound he had received in his head, which he'd thought fully healed. But now... in addition to the twitches he was having strange thoughts. Desires. Illicit desires.

He wondered if he and Elas Sil had done the right thing. But it was too late now. That sorceror, Bauchelain, was... frightening. In a peculiar, uncanny way. As if a warm thought had never once entered his mortal soul, and all that hid within was dark and cold. And the stories Imid had heard from the city up the coast... there was said to be a second sorceror, given to hiding, with the most venal appetites. Thus... *evil*.

A concept Imid had rarely thought about, but now it haunted him. There had been little particularly good about old Necrotus the Nihile. The usual assortment of unsavory indulgences common to those with absolute power. A score of repressive laws intended, as Elas Sil explained, to keep the king rich and free to revel in excess at the expense of the common folk. But if you paid your tithes and killed or robbed nobody important, you could live out your life without once crossing the path of trouble. And of course, such systemic corruption flowed down easily enough, the poison of cynicism infected the lowest city guard as much as it did the king. Bribery solved most problems, and where it couldn't, swift and brutal violence did. In other words, life was simple, straightforward and easily understood.

And, perhaps, *evil*. In the way of apathy, of indifference, of tacit acceptance of inhumanity. A cruel king made cruel nobles, who in turn made cruel merchants, and so on down to cruel stray dogs. And yet, Imid Factallo longed for a return to those times. For, it turned out, an earnest king, a king obsessed with goodness, delivered to all below him a certain zeal from which all manner of cruelty derived. Born of harsh judgmentalism—Elas Sil insisted such a word existed, and if didn't before then it did now—the sheer frenzy of noble ideals put into practice without flexibility or compassion was proving as destructive to the human spirit as anything Necrotus and his ilk may have contrived to inflict upon the people.

Evil possessed myriad faces, and some of them were open and genuine.

Whilst others, like Bauchelain's, revealed nothing, nothing at all.

Imid could not decide which of the two was more frightening.

He arrived at the home of Elas Sil, knocked thrice as custom dictated, then entered, as the law now permitted since privacy invited . . . private things. Entered, then, to find her quickly emerging from the curtained backroom, adjusting her tunic with a decidedly guilty expression on her face.

Imid stopped two steps in from the doorway, frozen in horror. "Who's back there?" he demanded. "He'll get castrated! And you—you—"

"Oh be quiet, there's no one back there."

He stared at her. "You were masturbating! That's illegal!"

"Nobody's ever proved the unhealthiness of it, have they?"

"Not physically, no, but emotionally unhealthy! Is there any doubt of that, Elas Sil? Your mind is drawn into base desires, and base desires lead to sordid appetites and sordid appetites leads to temptation and temptation leads to—"

"The end of civilisation. I know. Now, what do you want, Imid?"

"Well, uh, I was coming here to, uh, confess."

She advanced on him, smelling of women's parts, and with a growing sneer said, "Confess, Imid Factallo? And what must you confess to a fellow saint, if not *temptations*? You hypocrite!"

"I confess my hypocrisy! There, satisfied? I'm having . . . impulses. All right?"

"Oh, never mind," Elas said, turning away and sitting down on a nearby chair. "It's all so pathetic, isn't it? Did you hear? They're stealing babies, now. If it screams, it's breaking the law. If children play-fight in the street, they're breaking the law." She looked over. "Have you done your required exercises today?"

"No."

"Why is your face twitching?"

"I don't know. Must be a side effect."

"Of good living?"

"Oh, aren't you funny."

"Well, should we exercise together?"

Imid's eyes narrowed. "What do you have in mind?"

"Something seriously illegal. Your visit interrupted me."

"That's not exercise!"

"Now there's a depressing confession for you to make, Imid Factallo. Of course, I could take it as a challenge."

"You're disgusting." He paused. "Say some more disgusting things."

EMANCIPOR REESE WAS sweating by the time he passed unaccosted through the city gate. His nerves were jumping wildly and he felt slightly sick. Likely the dust and the stench of ox and mule sweat, he told himself as he jostled among the farmers driving their loaded carts through the narrow passage. With Oponn's blessing, he would have completed his tasks by tomorrow, and so could return to a sane lifestyle—or, as sane as was possible whilst in the employ of two homicidal masters.

He hoped his wife was living well on his earnings back in Lamentable Moll. The brats would be in school, still, although the eldest might well be apprenticed out by now. It had been four years, after all. A lifetime, given what the manservant had lived through since that fateful drunken day when he'd knocked on the door to Bauchelain's room at Sorrowman's Hostel.

She'd have found lovers by now, too, he suspected. Sailors, fishers, maybe even a soldier or two. He didn't begrudge that, much. It could be a lonely life, being a mother with no husband close by.

Twenty paces in from the gate, Emancipor moved off to stand clear of the carts and braying beasts of burden filing past. He looked round, trying to sense what was different about this place, compared to the countless other cities he had visited. It was quieter, for one thing. Off to the right, at the end of a narrow passage, was something like a square, in which citizens stood in rows waving their arms about and jumping in place. He wondered if these people might also be saints, all of them skull-cracked and now entirely insane. There were few urchins to be seen, and none of the hopelessly destitute begging for coins in the gutters. Indeed, the street looked surprisingly clean.

If this was the good life, then it wasn't so bad, he concluded.

Of course, it was not going to last. Not with Bauchelain and Korbal Broach scheming its downfall. He felt a pang of regret.

"What are you doing here?"

Emancipor turned. "Excuse me?"

The woman standing before him was wearing white enameled armour, a white cape lined in gold silk. Her face belonged to that of a marble statue carved by some artist obsessed with perfection, down to the pallid dust on her cheeks and to either side of her even, pert nose. The red paint glistening from her lips made it appear she had just drunk a flagon of blood. Cold, hard blue eyes were fixed on his with haughty contempt. "You're loitering, citizen."

"Actually, I was hesitating."

She blinked, then frowned. "Is there a difference?"

"Of course," Emancipor replied. He considered explaining the difference, then decided not to.

"Well," she finally said, "we don't like hesitation much, either."

"Then I will be on my way."

"Yes, but first, where are you going? By your accent you are some sort of foreigner—don't deny it! And we have concerns about foreigners. They possess unruly ideas. I need to know everything about you, beginning with your reason for coming to Quaint. Now, start talking!"

Her tirade had attracted onlookers, all of whom now turned with unveiled suspicion to Emancipor to await his answer.

Sweat beaded Emancipor's wrinkled brow. It should have been Bauchelain answering these damned questions. Or, even more amusing, Korbal Broach—with those flat, beady eyes, that flabby, placid smile. Inspiration struck the manservant, and he swung a glazy look on the fierce woman. "Who are you? My head hurts. Where are we?"

Her scowl deepened. "I was the one asking the questions."

"What has happened?" Emancipor asked. "I woke up outside the gate. I think. I was . . . I was working. Yes, I was working, with a crew, clearing a drainage ditch. There was this big rock, they wanted it moved—I was straining. Then—pain! In my head! By the Lady, I don't even know who I am!"

A gasp from the crowd. Then, *"He is a Saint!"*

The woman asked, "Have you been proclaimed by a Well Knight?"

"Uh, I don't think so. I don't remember. Maybe. What day is this?"

Someone in the crowd answered, "Saint Ebar's Day, oh chosen one!"

"Seven months!" Emancipor exclaimed. Then cursed himself. That was too long. What was he thinking?

"Seven months?" The Well Knight stepped closer. *"Seven months?"*

"I—I think so," Emancipor stammered. "What year is this?" Idiot! He was making it worse!

"The Second Year of the Rule of Macrotus."

"Macrotus!" the manservant exclaimed. Blathering fool, stop this! Now! Another inspiration. Emancipor rolled his eyes up, groaned, and collapsed onto the cobbles. Shouts from the crowd, figures moving close.

Conversations.

"Is he the one, then?"

"The very first Saint of Glorious Labour? He said seven years, didn't he? I'm sure he did. *Seven!*"

The Well Knight growled then, and said, "The myth of the First Saint—I mean, we have looked and looked and never found him, or her. Besides, this man's a foreigner. The First Saint cannot be a foreigner."

"But, Blessed Knight of Wellness," someone persisted, "all that he said fits! The First Saint, the harbinger of all that was to come! The Royal Prophecies—"

"I know the Royal Prophecies, citizen!" the woman snapped. "Careful, lest I conclude you are arguing loudly in a public place!"

A voice from further out, stentorian. "What is happening here?"

The woman replied with some relief. "Ah, Invett Loath. If you would be so kind, please assist in the adjudication of this situation."

The man's voice came closer. "Situation? Situations are frowned upon, Storkul Purge. Even a low-ranking Well Knight such as you must know this."

"I endeavour to promulgate conformity at every turn, Oh Purest of the Paladins."

"And well you should, lest by your actions you prove singular or, Lady forgive us, unique. You do not deem yourself unique, do you, Storkul Purge?"

Her voice was suddenly small. "Of course not. The purity of my innate mediocrity is absolute, Purest. Of that I can assure you."

"What is happening here? Who is this unconscious man?"

The persistent citizen was quick to answer, "The First Saint, Purest Paladin of Wellness! A man without memory, for the last seven years!"

"Then why is he unconscious?"

"He succumbed to the Well Knight's questioning. It was . . . shocking. Blessed be the Lady that you have arrived!"

No retort nor refutation came from the hapless Storkul Purge, and, lying at her very feet, Emancipor felt a surge of sympathy. That quickly went away. Let her roast, he concluded. And opened his eyes—immediately noticed—then fixed them on Storkul Purge. Another groan, another apparent plunge into oblivion.

"She did it again!" the citizen said in a gasp.

"Excuse yourself, Storkul Purge," Invett Loath commanded, "and await the Knightly Judgment at the Day Temple of Wellness."

A muted, "Yes, Purest Paladin."

Emancipor heard her boots scuff away.

"Awaken, First Saint," Invett Loath said.

This was perfect. Emancipor's eyes fluttered open. Bewildered, then resting with apparent recognition on the beat-stained, chiseled features of the armoured Knight standing over him. "I—I have never seen you before," the manservant said, "yet I know the purity of your soul. You must be the Paladin. You must be Invett Loath."

A gleam of pleasure lit the man's sharp blue eyes. "You are correct, First Saint. There is a little known prophecy that I would be the one to find you, and deliver you to our king. Are you well enough to stand?"

Emancipor struggled to his feet. Tottered momentarily and was steadied by a gauntleted hand.

"Come, First Saint of Most Glorious Labour—"

The manservant's knees buckled, forcing the Paladin to quickly clutch at him.

"What is it, my friend?" Invett Loath asked in alarm.

Ignoring the massive crowd surrounding them, Emancipor straightened once more, then leaned close to the Paladin. "A—a vision, Oh Purest. A terrible vision!"

"This is fell indeed! What have you seen?"

Emancipor lifted his head slightly. He would have to think of something, and fast. "For the ears of you and the King and none other!"

"Not even the Grand Nun of the Lady?"

"Oh, yes. Her too."

"Then we must be away. Here, take my arm . . . ."

WELL KNIGHT STORKUL PURGE leaned against the back wall of the Day Temple, staring sightlessly as waves of dread swept through her. She was doomed. Knightly Judgments never favored the judged. She had participated in them enough times to know that as an unmitigated truth, and she well recalled the secret visceral pleasure when adding her voice to the chorus of condemnation. Crimes against Wellness were without question the most serious offences these days, and that seriousness was only getting more serious. She frowned at that thought, then shook her head, suddenly fearful that she was losing her mind.

Then again, perhaps that was for the best. Insanity like a cocoon wrapped about herself before the moment of adjudication.

Damn that Invett Loath! Every Well Knight knew that the myth of the First Saint was an invention. The foreigner was little more than a quick-witted opportunist, clever enough to make mockery of treasured superstition whilst, at the same time, stroke Loath's ego. If anyone deserved adjudication, it was the Paladin of Purity, stomping about the city in the blinding cloud of his unsullied righteousness, a cloud thick enough to choke the fittest citizen.

Ah, did she have something there? Had not Invett Loath set himself above all others? Was he too not bound to conformity and secure mediocrity? Dare she challenge him?

"He will devour me alive," she whispered. "Who am I fooling? He's already sharpening the spike for me on the wall. By the Lady, I need a drink!" Her mouth shut with a click of teeth at that exclamation. Looking about, she saw, with relief, that no one was close.

Then, a small, raspy voice whispered, "Did someone mention a drink?"

Storkul Purge's head snapped round. The voice seemed to have come right beside her, but there was no one there. "Who spoke?" she demanded.

"I've caught a most delicious trail."

The Well Knight looked down, and saw a small, gaudily dressed shape lying beside her right boot.

The thing sniffed. "Do you not recognise me, Storkul Purge? Granted, these clothes ill fit me. T'was a dancer, a twirling, spinning celebrant—"

"You fool," Storkul said, sneering, "those clothes belonged to a puppet. I can still see the strings."

In a small voice, the thing said, "A puppet? Oh! I'm wasting away!"

"You are Vice," she said. "You are Ineb Cough. Why aren't you dead yet?"

"Oh, you don't understand! It was all I could manage to crawl to you! The lure of your desire—I heard it!"

"You are mistaken—"

"Ah, a lie! Good! Yes, lies are good. Lies are where I begin!"

"Be quiet! People will hear."

"Better and better. Yes, we will whisper, you and I. A drink, yes? Spirits, yes? I have caught a trail, leading out through Inland Gate. A trail, I tell you, redolent with all manner of indulgences. Liquor, rustleaf, durhang—"

"Inland Gate? Why, I was just there!"

"Someone has entered the city, my dear...."

"Someone? A foreigner? Yes, a foreigner!" She knew it!

"We must backtrack along his trail, you and me, Storkul Purge. We must!"

She was silent, thinking. Visions raced through her mind. Dramatic pronouncements, scenes of triumph at the fall of both the foreigner and Invett Loath. But it would not do to act too quickly. No, the two must become further entwined, each the champion of the other in their grand deceit. Yes, she could see it now. Soon, there would be a new champion of purity in Quaint.

But first.... "Very well, Ineb Cough, backtrack we shall."

"Delicious! Pick me up, then, my dark-hearted woman. Through Inland Gate, onto the open road beyond!"

"Quiet! You're getting too loud!" She reached down and collected the puny creature that was Ineb Cough. "Say nothing more," she whispered, "until I tell you it's safe."

Approaching the gate, she saw a guard step out, his eyes on her. "Well Knight, what have you there?"

"A most horrible child," she replied. "Infected."

The man edged back slightly. "Infected?"

"Children are not innocent, only inexperienced. It is a common enough misapprehension. This one is loud, boisterous, aggressive and cares only for itself."

"A singular child, then."

As any mother would tell you, you stupid mule-turd, I just described every child in this world. "Indeed, so singular we have no choice but to remove him bodily from the city."

"And what do you mean to do with him?" the guard asked.

"Leave him to the wolves. Launch him in a basket on the outgoing tide. Sell him to pernicious but unsuspecting slavers. I have not yet decided, guard. Now, if you would stand aside, lest the vapours of this wretched imp poison you...."

The guard took another step back, then waved her on with a nervous gesture.

Once out on the road, she paused. "All right, no one's close. Which way?"

"Straight ahead," Ineb replied, "forty paces, then left on the drover's track, up the hill. The very top. Gods below, the scent is strong and oh so lovely!"

Her basest desires urged her every step onward. Very disturbing. True, she'd once been, long ago, a most indulgent creature, sweet seductress in service to this very demon tucked under her arm. Like honey in a wasp trap, a furry mouse in a snake-pit, a whore at the temple backdoor. And it had been a good, if toxic, life. She admitted that she missed those days, rather, those nights. Yet, had not that foreigner and Invett Loath conspired her imminent downfall, she knew she would have gone on in her new, unstained life as a Knight of Wellness, pure of thought—all right, most of the time—and in the pious straits of healthy living. Respected and feared, representative and exalted far above the miserable mass of wretches crowding Quaint's streets. Wretches deserving little more than her sneering contempt.

And there was a little known truth. Healthy pursuits should have noticeably extended lives by now, but the sheer stress of the endeavour was killing people like mayflies. Clearly, your average citizen wasn't up to the task of living well. Victims of exercise and too many vegetables. Beneficence was a costly glory, it turned out. The chirurgeons were reporting that the most common complaint these days was blocked bowels. "And there you have it," she muttered under her breath as she climbed the drover's track, "what this city needs is a good dump, hah."

"For starters," Ineb Cough replied. "Yes indeed, a good clearing out of the system. An explosive expulsion of—"

"That's enough from you," Storkul said in a growl. "I was talking to myself."

The demon sniffed in a muffled fashion, "Didn't sound like it to me."

"Well, I was."

"Fine, but that's not what I heard, that's all."

"You heard wrong."

The creature spasmed under her arm, gaudy limbs writhing. "All right! I'm sorry! I'm sorry!"

"That," said a third voice, "was well done."

It originated from the summit, three strides ahead. Storkul Purge halted, stared up at the man. "What?" she asked. "What was well done?"

"You are a ventriloquist, yes? A fascinating profession, I have always thought, fraught with arcane sorcery and strange mental peculiarity—"

"She's not a ventriloquist," Ineb Cough snarled, still thrashing about.

The grey-bearded, elegantly dressed man almost smiled. "Please, ah, *both* of you—I am a most appreciative audience and you will be pleased at the gratuity I shall pay you for the performance."

"I am Well Knight Storkul Purge, *not* a caster of voices! Who are you and what are you doing here? Is that a camp on the summit behind you? Answer my questions, damn you, in the name of the Lady of Beneficence!"

"Answer her!" the demon added in a vicious rasp.

The man clapped his long-fingered hands. "Oh, very good indeed."

Knight and demon howled their outrage.

"Spectacular!"

Storkul Purge flung the demon down and advanced on the man. Flopping in the dust behind her, Ineb Cough screamed, "I smell rustleaf!"

The stranger took a step back, thin brows rising. "Exquisite drama," he said. "And highest sorcery, since I do not see the strings—"

"Silence, you wretched cur!" She saw the wagon at the far edge of the summit, and two bone-white oxen lolling stupidly as oxen were wont to do—although as both beasts swung their heads to regard her, the Knight faltered upon seeing their onyx black eyes. Nearby was the remnant of a cook fire, and lying close to the ring of stones were two wine bottles. "Alcohol! As I suspected!" She rounded on the foreigner. "Ignorance of the prohibitions is not an acceptable defense! I should have you arrested and—"

"A moment," the man interrupted, lifting one finger, which he then set to his bearded chin. "Whilst ignorance of prohibitions may not be an acceptable defense, what of ignorance of what constitutes an acceptable defense?"

"What?"

"And what of your ignorance of the proper charge to be made against me?" the man inquired, the finger now tapping a steady rhythm. "Do you have an acceptable defense regarding that?"

"I *know* which are the proper charges!"

"Then why are you being so vague about them?"

"I'm not being vague!"

"Ahh," he said with a slight smile, and the finger wagged lazily.

"Be quiet both of you!" the demon shrieked as it clawed its way to the summit. "Storkul Purge, have you forgotten your own desires? Forgotten what has brought us here?"

The Knight spun round and stared down at Ineb Cough, struggled against the impulse to crush him underfoot. Then, mastering herself, she faced the foreigner once more. "The demon is right. I am not here in the capacity of a Knight of Wellness."

"A Knight of Wellness? I see," the foreigner said, slowly nodding. Then his placid gaze slid down to Ineb Cough. "And a demon in truth, although much diminished. Mind you, well suited to ornamental functions. Had I a mantle piece . . . alas, such are the vicissitudes of travel."

"*A mantle piece*," the demon hissed in outrage. "I was once a giant! The Tyrant of Hedonism! That's what they called me. The Demon of Vice, you damned conjurer, had no equal! They all bowed to me—Corpulence, Sloth, even Lust!"

"You were manifest in Quaint?" the man asked. "How extra-ordinary. Whomever was responsible for you displayed exquisite extravagance—I would have liked to meet that woman."

Storkul Purge cocked her head. "Woman? How do you know it was a woman?"

The man eyed her for a moment, then he turned away. "Come, my friends, join me at this modest hearth. Here, in my manservant's pack, we shall find no modest supply of illegal condiments, I am certain." A gesture towards the heap of ashes, the flicker of magic—

A nearby bush burst into flames.

The man started. "My humblest apologies. That was unin-tended, I assure you." He gestured again, and wood appeared in the hearth, heat curling and sudden snaps announcing ignition. In the meantime the bush still raged, throwing up strangely colored tongues of fire. Eyeing it askance, Storkul Purge edged closer to the hearth. Behind her, Ineb Cough crawled with minute grunts and gasps—he seemed to be heading for the wine bottles.

"Do not think," the Knight said, "I am here with the inten-tion of imbibing in unwholesome habits."

"Unwholesome, you say," the man said, his broad forehead wrinkling in a frown as he rummaged through the frayed leather sack. "Certainly a matter of opinion. I favour wine for the most part, and consider it salubrious and, in moderation, enlivening. As such, nothing unwholesome."

"It deadens the brain," she replied harshly. "Indeed, kills it minutely, in increments. More pernicious than that, it assaults the blood and loosens natural discipline."

"Natural discipline? Gods below, what a peculiar notion!"

"Nothing peculiar to it," she said. "It is the mechanism employed by the instinctive desire for health."

"As opposed to well-being."

"Health and well-being are not in opposition."

"A fierce pronouncement, Miss Purge. Oh, I have been rude.

I am Bauchelain. As you see me, no more than a gentle traveler, with no intention—no, none indeed—of settling in your fair city."

"What is with your oxen, Bauchelain?" she demanded. "Those eyes . . . . "

"A rare breed—"

Ineb Cough snorted as he clambered onto the first wine bottle, head thrust out, tiny tongue poking towards the bottle's neck. "Ynah. Nhn. Yhn." His tongue flicked cat-like against the dark, pocked glass.

"Here we are," Bauchelain said, drawing forth a number of objects. "Rustleaf. Durhang, in dried leaf form, in soft ball form. White nectar—where in Hood's realm did he come by that, I wonder? Uthurl poppy . . . hmm, an assortment of medicines all sharing the theme of stupor, employed to calm highly beset nerves. I had no idea my phlegmatic manservant suffered such ailments. And here, some wine. And peach liquor, and pear liquor, and here is some whale sperm—Queen of Dreams, what does he do with that, I wonder? No matter, we are each and all mysterious miracles in our own ways, yes? Now, I am certain Mister Reese will not begrudge your partaking of his prodigious supply—imbibe as you desire. I myself shall sample some of this Falari wine . . . . "

Storkul Purge stared down at the vast array of prohibited substances. A small whimper escaped her.

*B*EYOND THE FORMAL entrance was a long, wide colon-nade lined on each side with upright corpses set in coffins. The lids were glass, murky and bubbled but not, alas, sufficient to disguise the inhabitants. Positioned between narrow, marble columns, a host of blurry, shrunken eyes seemed to track Emancipor and Invett Loath as they made their way down the vast hallway. A set of double doors waited at the far end.

"The Healthy Dead," the Paladin of Purity said, one arm still taking most of the manservant's weight. "As you can see, they are all well. Clean of spirit and hale. Glorious evidence of the rewards that come with living unsullied by the foul indulgences that once cursed our people."

"Why are they all grimacing?" Emancipor asked.

"The Lady takes most mortals unto her bosom by maladies of the colon."

"Death by constipation?"

"The zeal of health. Many citizens eat grass to excess."

"Grass?"

"Have you no memory of such things? No, how could you? Having been made a Saint in the time of Necrotus the Nihile. Indeed, grass, a fine substitute for meat. Our chirurgeons have dissected all manner of corpses—early on, they often slit open stomachs to find solid pieces of meat, resident in undigested fashion for years in the victim. Truly horrific. Now, of course, they find knotted bundles of grass, which as you might imagine is a far less disgusting discovery—after all, cows die of that all the time."

"And now, cows and citizens both."

"You'd be surprised, First Saint, at the similarities."

Emancipor glanced up to see something dark and satisfied in the Paladin's flushed face. After a moment, Invett Loath resumed, "Peruse this corpse, here . . . that one, for a moment." They halted before one of the coffins. "See the even pallour? See how shiny all that newly grown hair is? This, my friend, is a thing of beauty, a monument to supreme healthiness."

"I couldn't agree more," Emancipor said, staring in fascination at the fixed pain-wracked expression on the poor lady's face behind the blue-green glass. "I imagine her relatives are very proud to have her here in the palace."

"Oh no," Invett Loath said, "not in the least. Madness struck them one and all upon her death—I tell no lie when I say that their lust for meat led them to eat most of her left leg—yes, the wrapped one. Thus, the rest of her family will be found on the spikes."

Emancipor stared at the Paladin, aghast. "What could drive loved ones to do such a thing?"

"Moral weakness, First Saint. It is a plague, ever ready to spread its infection upon the citizens, and this is the greatest responsibility of the Well Knights, to ensure that such weakness is rooted out and mounted high on the walls. And I can tell you, we are as busy today as we were a year ago, perhaps busier."

"No wonder there are so few people on the streets."

"Diligence, First Saint. An unending demand, but we are equal to it."

They resumed their journey down the cavernous hall. "But not that . . . woman who first accosted me," Emancipor said.

"Storkul Purge? I've had my eye on her for some time. She was a prostitute, did you know that? Before the Prohibitions. A fallen woman, a creature of disgusting vices, a seductress of dreadful hedonism, a singular threat to civilisation—her conversion was so sudden that I was instantly suspicious. We have done well, you and I, to expose her inequities. She shall suffer adjudication, this very night."

Emancipor winced, overwhelmed by a flood of guilt. "Can there be no second chance, Paladin?"

"Ah, you are a saint indeed, to voice such sentiment. The answer is no, there cannot. The very notion of fallibility was invented to absolve mortals of responsibility. We can be perfect, and you can see true perfection walking here at your side."

"You have achieved perfection?"

"I have. I am. And to dispute that truth is to reveal your own imperfection."

They arrived at the double doors. Invett Loath reached for the large rings—but the door on the right suddenly opened, the edge cracking against the Paladin's nose with a wet crunching sound. The man reeled back, blood spurting.

Emancipor stumbled, then, his boot settling on a smear of blood, he lost his balance and pitched forward, through the open door, where he struck a dumbfounded servant, his head sinking into the woman's belly.

Breath exploded from her and, as Emancipor fell face first onto the floor, she collapsed onto him, the large bowl perched on her head wheeling away, a brain-sized mass of wet grass heaving into the air like a thing alive to splat and slide in runny mint sauce across the tiles—

—directly beneath Invett Loath's left boot as he stepped down. The Paladin skidded, landed with a solid thump on his backside.

Groaning, Emancipor pushed the woman off, then rolled onto his side. In the hallway behind him, he could hear Invett Loath's spattering gasps. Beside the manservant, the servant dragged in her first breath after a long moment of eye-bulging, gaping panic. And, somewhere in the chamber beyond, there came to Emancipor's ears a strange mechanical sound, repeating in steady, indifferent rhythm. Blinking tears from his eyes, he climbed to his hands and knees and looked up.

A massive, iron-framed, hinged and wheeled and cabled contraption dominated the chamber, and in its midst, bound by straps and padded shackles, there was a figure. Suspended an arm's length above the floor, limbs gyrating incessantly, as if the man was climbing air, trapped in place, his shaggy-haired head slowly lolling in time with the various fulcrums and pulleys and ratcheting gears.

The mechanism was so large there was no way to get close to the figure hanging in its centre, and with his back to the doors, it was clear that King Macrotus—for who else could it be?—had heard nothing of the commotion at the entrance. He exercised on, unceasing, steadily, a man in perpetual motion.

Invett Loath staggered through the doorway, his face streaked with blood running down the nostrils of his broken nose. He spat, pain-pinched eyes fixing upon the servant who still sat on the floor. "Whore's beget! Slayer of civilisation! I shall adjudicate you here and now!"

To this bellow King Macrotus paid no visible attention, arms rising in turn, legs pumping in counterpoint—the man looked frighteningly thin, yet strangely flaccid, as if his skin had lost all elasticity.

Emancipor clambered upright. "Paladin of Purity, it was an accident!"

"Accidents are signs of weakness!"

Invett Loath, the manservant could see, was in a hot, blinding rage. "'Ware your words!" Emancipor snapped.

The huge man wheeled on him, red jaw dropping.

Heart pounding, Emancipor stabbed out an accusing finger. "Do you condemn this city's Saints of Glorious Labour, Paladin? One and all? Victims of accidents, are they not? Dare you adjudicate in defiance of *my* people? Before our beloved king himself?"

Invett Loath stepped back. "Of course not!" Eyes flicked to Macrotus in his harness, then back to Emancipor. "But she is little more than a wench—"

"Serving the king himself!" Emancipor said. "Moreover, she has been injured...whilst," he added with sudden inspiration, "conducting glorious labour!" The manservant reached down to settle his hand on the trembling woman's head. "She is now a Saint!"

"Such proclamation," the Paladin said, "must be sanctioned by a Well Knight...."

"Indeed, by none other than you, Invett Loath. Is King Macrotus to witness hesitation?"

"No! I do hereby sanctify this woman as a Saint of Glorious Labour!"

Emancipor helped the woman to her feet. Close to her ear, he whispered, "Get out of here, lass. Quick!"

She bowed, collected her bowl, then scurried away.

Emancipor found a handkerchief in a pocket and handed it up to the Paladin, watched as Invett cleaned up his face, wiping the cloth back and forth, then again, back and forth. And again, back and forth beneath the suddenly glittering, suddenly wide eyes. Slowly, shock filled the manservant.

That handkerchief...D'bayang poppy spores...oh dear.... "Paladin, the King seems indisposed at the moment...."

"As always," Invett Loath said in an odd, jumpy voice. "But yes. Too busy. Exercising. Exercising. Up down up down down up down exercise! We've tallied too long. Lethargy is a sin. Let us get going." He held the cloth to his nose again. "Exercise. I need to patrol the streets. All of them, yes, by dusk. I can do that. You don't believe me? I'll show you!"

The Paladin charged out of the chamber.

And Emancipor found himself alone.

With King Macrotus. Who exercised on, and on.

"THESE CLOTHES ARE too tight," Ineb Cough complained.

"You have burgeoned some," Bauchelain observed. "Here, have more wine, my friend."

"Yes, very good. I will. But I'm feeling . . . constricted."

Nearby, Storkul Purge paced, a woman at war with herself. Ineb was disappointed that she still resisted the delicious lure of all these wondrous condiments. Taking another mouthful from the bottle, the demon edged closer to Bauchelain. "Sorceror," he whispered, then smiled, "Oh yes, I know you for what you are. You and that crow circling overhead. Necromancers! Tell me, what are you doing here?"

Bauchelain glanced over at the Well Knight, then fixed his regard on the demon. He stroked his bearded chin. "Ah, now, that is something of a mystery, isn't it?"

"That manservant you mentioned. He's in the city, isn't he? Purchasing supplies for your journey? Perhaps, but more than that, I suspect." Ineb smiled again. "I can smell conspiracies, oh yes."

"Can you now? I would ask you, where are your fellow demons?"

"In some alley, I expect. Except for Agin Again—she's disappeared."

"Agin Again?"

"The Demoness of Lust."

"Disappeared? For how long, Ineb Cough?"

"Around the time of Necrotus's sudden demise."

"And how soon, upon taking the crown, did Macrotus announce the prohibitions?"

"These clothes are strangling me!"

Bauchelain reached down. "Allow me to un-do those buttons—oh, they're just for show. I see. Well, shall I cut you free?"

"No. Another drink would be better. Yes. Excellent. The prohibitions? About a week, during which he'd already begun . . . preparing the way. Elevating the Lady of Beneficence to the official religion. If you think on it, that act foreshadowed all that followed. A newly recruited army of piety, sanctioned to police the behaviour of every citizen in Quaint. By the Abyss, we should have seen it coming!" Yanking at his collar, Ineb stole another glance over at Storkul Purge, then leaned even closer to the sorceror. "You're planning something, yes? What? Tell me!"

"I was considering removing, from your companion, a certain quantity of blood."

The demon stared at the sorceror, then licked his lips. "Oh. How . . . how much blood did you have in mind?"

Bauchelain had picked up the bottle of whale sperm and was studying it. "Well, that depends on its purity."

"Ah, I see. It must needs be pure. I think, Bauchelain, that her blood is very pure indeed. Given that . . . are we talking a fatal amount?"

The sorceror's brows rose. He raised the bottle and peered at the thick sediments at the base, then gave it a shake. "Difficult to say, alas. Oh look, they're still alive—how can that be? I am no longer convinced this sperm belonged to a whale. No, not at all. Curious."

"Were you planning on asking her for it?"

Surprise flitted across the sorceror's ascetic features. "Ask? I admit I had not thought of that."

"And this blood," Ineb said, pulling himself into a tightly bound crouch, "what do you intend on doing with it?"

"Me? Nothing. My traveling companion, however, shall employ it in a ritual of resurrection."

The demon scanned the sky, seeking sight of the crow. It wasn't around at the moment. He shifted uneasily. "Resurrection. Of course, why didn't I think of that? I can answer that question. I couldn't because you won't tell me what you're planning."

"Nothing dramatic, I assure you. The overthrow of King Macrotus. We shall endeavour to preserve as much of the city's population as possible."

"You want Quaint's throne?"

"For ourselves? Hardly. What would we do with it? No, consider it a favour."

"A favour?"

"Very well, we are being paid to achieve the swift extinction of this deadly trend toward healthiness. Although, truth be said, I am not much interested in material wealth. Rather, it is the challenge that intrigues me." Bauchelain straightened and faced Storkul Purge. After a moment, the sorceror drew out a knife.

IMID FACTALLO'S LIFE had never amounted to much, thus far. Such was his considered opinion in any case. No wife, no children, and he not a man women would chase, unless he'd stolen something from them. And so he'd known loneliness, as familiar as an old friend, in fact. Although, presumably, to have a friend was to be other than lonely. Thinking on that, he was forced to conclude that loneliness was not anything like an old friend. Indeed, had he a friend, he would have been able to discuss his thoughts, since that's what friends did, and clearly the conversation would have been scintillating.

He sat on the front step of his modest, friendless abode, watching a squirrel twitch confusedly at the base of a tree. It had been busy for weeks storing various things in anticipation of the winter to come. Curiously, it seemed such rodents despised company. Loneliness was their desired state. This is what came, he concluded morosely, of eating nuts and seeds.

The creature's present confusion had no outwardly apparent cause, suggesting to Imid that the source of its troubles came from within, a particular cavort of agitation in its tiny brain. Perhaps it was experiencing an ethical crisis, making it jump about so in chittering rage.

All the fault of that damned manservant, Imid told himself. Mulled wine and rustleaf and durhang, a veritable cornucopia of forbidden substances, and his indifferent aplomb in the consumption of those items had taken Imid's breath away. Cruel as a squirrel, he'd been. Driving the Saint of Glorious Labour to distraction, and worse ... thoughts of violence.

He became aware of a susurration of noise from down the street, in the direction of the Grand Temple of the Lady. A crowd. Distant screams.

Imid Factallo saw the squirrel freeze in its tracks, head cocked. Then it fled.

The sounds were getting louder.

The saint leaned out slightly, peering down the street.

More screams, shattering pottery, a heavy crash—he saw a mass of motion, filling the space between the buildings. A mob, in full charge now, coming this way.

Alarmed, Imid Factallo rose from the step.

A hundred citizens, maybe more. Faces twisted in terror and panic, Saints of Glorious Labour among them. And worthies. And nuns—what was this?

They swept opposite Imid where he stood, clawing each other, clambering over those who fell. A wailing baby rolled to the bottom step, directly below Imid, and he snatched it clear a moment before a worthy's boot slammed down on that spot. Staggering backward until his shoulders struck the door behind him, Imid stared as the mob surged past.

And, in its wake, the Paladin of Purity, Invett Loath. He'd drawn his sword, the polished steel flashing as he waved the weapon above his head, marching as if leading a parade. Or driving sheep.

"Weaklings!" the Paladin bellowed. "Run, you assorted pieces of filth! You are all being adjudicated! I have seen your faces! Smelled your foul breaths! Unclean, all of you! None of you shall escape my judgment!"

Noting Imid standing with the now-silent babe in his arms, Invett Loath pointed his sword at them. "You are witness!"

Imid stared. In his arms, the babe stared. From the rooftop directly overhead, the squirrel stared.

In Invett's other hand was a handkerchief, which the Paladin used to wipe dried blood from his face. The man's eyes glittered, appallingly bright. "Announce yourselves! Witnesses! Or suffer the fate of the Impure!"

"We witness!" Imid squealed. The babe wisely added a bubbling burble.

Triumphant, the Paladin of Purity marched on, driving his flock ever onward.

Something near the Grand Temple was burning, smoke twisting and billowing in dark, almost black clouds.

A figure approached in the wake of Invett Loath, and Imid was startled to see Elas Sil, moving furtively towards him.

"Elas Sil!"

"Quiet, you fool! Did you see him? He's gone mad!" She paused. "That baby's not yours!"

"I never said it was."

"Then why are you holding it? Don't you know how dangerous that is? It might void, it might wail, or worst of all, thrash about!"

"Someone dropped it."

"On its head?" She came closer and peered at it. "That smudge—is that a bruise?"

"It might be—"

"By the Lady, is this a Saint? Imid, you have discovered the youngest Saint of Glorious Labour!"

"What? It's just a baby—"

"A Saint!"

"What labour? Babies don't work! Elas Sil, you've lost your senses!"

"Look at its face, you fool—it's working right now!"

Something warm squelched against Imid's lap, and then the stench struck him.

☿

53

In the meantime, the mob of the adjudicated had grown. Four hundred and twenty-six and counting, charging in a stampede up Greentongue Avenue. Whilst, on each side, down alleys and side streets, the riot spread like runny sewage.

A drover who had been leading thirty oxen to a seller's compound lost control of his terrified beasts. Moments later, they were thundering madly, straight into a number of heavily burdened wagons that had been backed up and were sitting directly beneath the Monument of Singe—an ancient solid brick edifice, twenty stories tall, of dubious origin and unknown significance.

Loaded onto the beds of the wagons were caskets of jellied oil, which had been sweating out the entire day, forming a glistening patina on the sodden wood. Arto the Famous Fire Eater, whose fame had dwindled to pathetic ashes of late, was passing by at that moment. He had time to turn and see the wall-eyed oxen stampeding towards him, then was struck by a massive horned head, the impact throwing him back, the stoke-pot slung from his right shoulder wheeling outward, spraying its coals in all directions.

The subsequent explosion was heard and felt by every citizen in Quaint, and those crews out in the bay, throwing four-finned fish from their nets, looked up in time to see the skyward pitching fireball and at least three oxen cart-wheeling above the city, before the Monument of Singe dropped from sight and flames lit the dust clouds a gaudy orange.

*B*AUCHELAIN SLOWLY WIPED the blood from his knife blade with a bleached cloth. He glanced down at Ineb Cough for a moment, then away, westward to where the sun was crawling down into its cave of night. Poised, like a figure in some heroic tapestry.

The demon was lying prone, trapped into immobility by the straits of the puppet's clothes.

"All right," Ineb growled, "cut me loose. But carefully!"

"You need have no concern there, demon," Bauchelain said, crouching down and extending the dagger. "However, if you continue to squirm . . . . "

"I won't move, I promise!"

The brief flapping of wings announced the crow's return. A pungent, musty smell wafted over Ineb, then a second figure appeared at Bauchelain's side. A huge man, bald, his skin the tone and pallour of a hard-boiled and peeled egg, likely as clammy to the touch, as well. Small, flat eyes regarded the demon with cold curiosity.

Ineb tried a toothy smile. "I know what you're thinking," he said. "But no. Not me. Not a homunculus. Not even a golem. I am a real demon."

The man licked his flabby lips.

Ineb fell silent, mouth suddenly dry.

The tip of the dagger slipped beneath the demon's jacket just above Ineb's straining belly. Began slicing upward.

Bauchelain lifted his other hand, offering his companion the bloodied cloth. "The sun has set, Korbal Broach," he said. A snip, and the jacket parted. The sorceror began working on the sleeves.

Korbal Broach took the cloth and held it to his face. He breathed deep, then, smiling, he turned away and walked off a short distance. He tossed the cloth down at his feet, made a few gestures in the air with his right hand, then faced Bauchelain and nodded.

"And the unclean ones, Korbal Broach?"

The man's round face pinched in disappointment, almost petulant.

"Ah, of course," Bauchelain murmured. "Forgive me, friend."

Three more cuts and the clothes fell from Ineb. The demon clambered upright and drew in a savage, satisfied lungful of air. "Excellent! Much better. I'm a new demon."

Storkul Purge staggered over. "I'm bleeding," she said in a high, wavering voice.

Ineb sneered at her. "He pricked your finger, woman!"

"I think I'm going to faint."

Bauchelain sheathed his knife. "Please, sit, Miss Purge. Ineb, pour the unwell Knight some wine."

*T*UNIC SODDEN AND FOUL, Imid Factallo ran down the street, Elas Sil at his side. The baby squirmed in his arms, but its expression was content.

Behind them, a long distance runner, returning from a six league sojourn out of the city and his mind understandably befuddled, ran into a burning building. And did not re-emerge. Panicked animals and frenzied citizens scampered in all directions through the smoke, sparks and ashes. The lamp-lighters had not appeared, leaving only the conflagrations in various districts of the city to fight against the encroaching darkness.

Elas clutched at Imid's arm and tugged. "This way!" Down a narrow, winding alley.

"Don't hurt us!" A piping, squealing cry from somewhere up ahead.

They halted, looked round in the gloom.

"Leave us be!"

Imid Factallo edged forward, eyeing the two small figures lying in the rubbish two paces in front of him. Absurdly tiny, the both of them. On the left, a man, his skin a mass of wrinkles, like a golden fig. Beside him, a woman, tiny but nonetheless a woman in the adult sense, as if some perverted inventor had fashioned a breastly, slim-legged doll upon which to lavish sick fantasies.

"Bridges of the Abyss," Elas Sil whispered. "What are these?"

The wrinkled one said, "I am Corpulence, known to my many friends as Nauseo Sloven. And my companion here is Sloth, Senker Later by name. And do I smell something?

Something . . . imminent? Enlivening? Oh yes I do. Can you smell it, Senker?"

"I can't be bothered to sniff."

"Ah yes! Ennui returns . . . belatedly!"

Imid Factallo said, "That smell would be baby turd."

"Not that. Something else. Something . . . wonderful."

Behind them, sudden shrieks sounded from the street.

"What was that?" Nauseo asked.

Elas Sil pulled Imid's arm again. "Let's get out of here."

They edged round the two demons.

"Where to?" Imid asked.

"Grand Temple. To hand the baby over to the nuns."

"Good idea. They'll know what to do with it."

In their wake, Nauseo Sloven crawled closer to the Demoness of Sloth. "I'm feeling better, did you know that? Better. It's strange. Changes are coming to Quaint, oh yes."

The screams came closer.

"We should run," Senker said.

"Run? Why?"

"Oh, you're right. Why bother?"

*E*MANCIPOR REESE WALKED out of the throne room. Although, truth be told, it could hardly be called a throne room, unless an iron-framed, geared and pulley-strapped mechanism as large as a room could be called a throne.

Then again, why not? Was not the apparatus of state a repetition of balances, weight and counter-weights? Of course it was. Metaphorically. With the king in the middle, burdened by birthright and suspended within a structure founded upon the delusional notion of hierarchical superiority. As if inequality could be justified in the name of tradition and the underlying assumptions were self-evident and therefore unassailable. And was not this zeal for fanatical health an identical delusion of superiority, this time bound to moral tenets? As if vigor was innately virtuous?

Sadly, it was part of the sordid nature of humanity, Emancipor reflected as he walked down the wide, long colonnade, to concoct elaborate belief systems all designed to feed one's own ego. And to keep those with less obnoxious egos in check. An unending multitude of daggers to hold against someone else's throat—

Shattering glass scattered his thoughts. Glinting shards falling inward on either side of the grand corridor. Strange and ghastly shapes clambering free—the healthy dead—climbing out from their upright coffins, hands grasping, clutching at the air. Horrible moaning sounds issued from desiccated, ravaged throats, mouths gaping wide. Staggering free, their cries growing louder, more desperate.

Emancipor Reese stared, then he groaned, and muttered, "Korbal Broach...."

A corpse reeled in front of him, its shriveled eyes seeming to fix on Emancipor. It wasn't as far gone as many of the others, and strange fluids were weeping down its flaccid cheeks. The jaw worked for a moment, creaking, then it said, *"It's all a lie!"*

"What is?"

"We go. All of us. To the same place. The healthy, the sickly, the murderers, the saints! All the same, terrible place! Crowded, so crowded!"

The dead, Emancipor had long since discovered, rarely had anything good to say. But even then, no two ever said the same thing. He admitted to a growing fascination for the details of the innumerable private nightmares death delivered. "What does it look like?" he now asked. "This crowded place?"

"A giant market," the corpse replied, fingers grasping at nothing. *"So much food. Treasures. So many...things!"*

"Well, that doesn't sound so bad."

"But I have no money!" This, a rasping shriek, and the corpse clawed at its own face, then wheeled away, moaning. *"No money. No money. No money. Everybody else has money—even the murderers! Why not me? Oh, why not meeee?"*

Emancipor stared after it.

A dead woman staggered past, seeming to reach down and lift up invisible objects. *"This one's not mine!"* she wailed. *"This one isn't either! Oh, where is my baby? Whose babies are these? Oh! Oh!"* She moved on, picking up and discarding more invisible babies. *"They're all so ugly! Who's responsible for all these ugly babies?"*

The colonnade was filled with wandering corpses now, although there was a general, almost haphazard convergence towards the outer doors. Emancipor suspected they would soon begin seeking out their living loved ones, since that was what the undead usually did, given the chance. Driven to utter last regrets, spiteful accusations or maundering mewling. Mostly pathetic, and only occasionally murderous. Nonetheless, this was to be a night, Emancipor surmised, that few in Quaint would ever forget.

"ABYSS BELOW," Imid Factallo whispered, "that man looks decidedly unhealthy."

Crouched in the shadows beside him, Elas Sil softly grunted, then hissed, "That's because he's dead, you idiot!"

The figure, stump-like feet dragging, was making its irregular way across the plaza that sprawled before the formal entrance to the Grand Temple. The concourse was littered with rubbish and ominous puddles, but, apart from the lone undead, deserted. Somewhere behind the temple's rearing bulk, some buildings were on fire, and glowing smoke billowed in the night sky. Screams and shrieks of terror reached them from all sides, every street and alley, from tenements and residences.

"What has happened?" Imid asked in a tremulous voice.

"Try using that healthy brain of yours, fool," Elas snapped. "This is *our* fault. You and me, Imid Factallo."

He blinked, then, eyes darting, he faced her. "But it was all the saints, all of us! We were just the ones to deliver the coins!" He stared out again at the stumping corpse. "They never said anything about, about, uh, raising the dead!"

"They're necromancers!"

"But how is this going to get rid of King Macrotus?"

"Hush! Are you mad? Not another word of that!"

Imid Factallo looked down at the baby, slumbering in his arms. "By the Lady," he whispered, "what have we done? What life will this child find here?"

"Oh relax," Elas Sil said, "those corpses will fall apart eventually. Then we'll just pick up the pieces . . . and bury them somewhere."

"Do you think," Imid asked, oddly breathless, "that *everyone* who was dead . . . ?"

Elas Sil eyed him sidelong. "Got some secrets, have you?"

"No! Nothing like that. Only, well, there was Mother . . . I mean, I loved her dearly, of course. But, still . . . . "

"Not charmed with the idea of seeing her again?" Elas gave him a particularly nasty smile, then snorted. "Well, you think you've got problems. I pushed my husband down the stairs."

Imid stared at her.

She laughed. "Aren't we the perfect saints!"

He looked out into the plaza. "Do you think—do you think he's out there?"

"Why wouldn't he be?"

"Why did you kill him?"

"He peed standing up."

"What?"

She glared. "It's messy, isn't it? I kept telling him to wipe the chute rim after. But did he? Never! Not once! Finally, well, I'd just had enough! Why are you looking at me like that? It was justifiable, a mercy killing, in fact. Imagine, being a man who can't aim! It must have been humiliating!"

"What, not peeing straight or never wiping up?"

"I had multiple arguments prepared, all sufficiently valid. Just in case the Guard got suspicious. But they weren't interested, not after I bribed them. This was in Necrotus's time, of course."

"Of course."

"Look, the way is clear. Let's go."

They rose from their hiding place and scurried out onto the concourse.

*I*NEB COUGH HOPPED from one leg to the other, eyes on the fires bathing the underside of smoke over the city. He shot Bauchelain a glance. "I'm sensing hunger in there. The desire to ... indulge!"

The sorceror nodded, his arms folded, and said, "That would be the *un*healthy dead."

Storkul Purge looked up with drunken suddenness. "But there is no alcohol in Quaint! Not a drop! And no rustleaf or durhang! No whores, no gambling establishments!"

Bauchelain smiled his half-smile. "My dear Knight, your naiveté is charming. How many floorboards are being pried up right now, I wonder? How many long-locked cellar doors are squealing open? And when the living see what their dead visitors have uncovered, all those well-hidden hoards, well, even a saint such as you will make the correct conclusions."

Ineb Cough capered over to squat beside Storkul Purge. "More wine?" he asked.

She held out her cup and Vice poured, careful not to spill a drop despite his burgeoning eagerness to return to Quaint's now or soon-to-be-delirious streets. When he was done he scampered away again, and noticed that Korbal Broach was nowhere to be seen, and indeed, Bauchelain was adjusting his cloak and examining the polish of his boots. "Blessed sorceror," Ineb said, "are you going somewhere?"

The man regarded him a moment, then nodded. "Oh yes. The time has come to enter your beloved city."

Ineb jumped up and down. "Excellent! Oh, it shall be such a fete! The living, the dead, everyone will be there!"

"Korbal Broach's work is done," Bauchelain murmured. "Now, mine begins . . . ."

Ineb Cough leapt to the man's side. He did not want to miss this.

Storkul Purge tottered to her feet and stood, wobbling. "Hurla's Brothel. It'll be re-opening for business. Hurla's dead, but that shouldn't matter. Much. Her clients won't know the difference. My room's still there—they'll be waiting for me. Oh, let's hurry!"

CLEARLY, EMANCIPOR OBSERVED, the veil of civilisation was thin indeed, so easily torn away to reveal depravity waiting beneath, waiting, as such things always did, for the first hint of turbulence. Even so, the burgeoning of anarchy was something to behold. The vast concourse fronting the palace was filled with figures, most of them dreadfully dead and in terrible states of decay. Which seemed little more than a minor inconvenience as they staggered about, waving dusty bottles in their bony hands, fluids leaking down their legs. One woman was sprawled on the palace steps, drawing rustleaf smoke in from a hookah, the smoke then swirling out through various rotted holes in her chest. A long-deceased prostitute chased an all-too-alive man through the crowds, demanding long overdue monies from some past transaction. His shrieks of remorse filled the air.

Citizens fought with dead relatives over possession of various indulgences, and in these cases the corpses usually fared worse, since the living were able to tear arms off and break brittle shins, which seemed an egregious thing to do to relatives, whether they deserved it or not. But now that the locks had been let loose on all manner of desires, the ensuing war was entirely understandable.

Still, Emancipor wondered as he stood at the top of the palace steps, it was all rather... sudden. The raising of the dead, healthy and unhealthy, should not have so easily triggered such a hedonistic conflagration. Had Bauchelain done something to add spice to the mix? Probably.

More buildings had caught fire, and the air was bitter with smoke and drifting ashes. He considered what to do next, then sat down on the rough stone. To stare out, bemused, on the macabre frenzy in the square.

INEB COUGH, BAUCHELAIN and Storkul Purge stood on the road before the city gates, staring up at the row of impaled figures on the wall. Animated yet spiked in place, their legs jerked and kicked about, heels cracking against the battered stone.

"I have seen," Bauchelain said, "a dance, in a far land, much like this."

"And are those dancers spiked to a wall, too?" Ineb asked.

"No, but they might as well have been. And indeed, as my manservant might concur, they *should* have been."

Ineb stared up at the row of kicking figures. Some had their hands on their hips. "I see his point," the demon said.

"Well," Bauchelain sighed, "there are no guards visible at the gate, suggesting that our entrance will not be challenged." The necromancer set off towards the rubbish-strewn passage. Then halted. "But first, I must fulfill a promise." He looked up at the wall again. "Ah, there he is." A gesture, and Ineb Cough watched as one of the dancing corpses lifted clear of its impaling spike, then slowly drifted down, still kicking and with its hands on its hips.

The corpse's mouth opened wide. "I can't stop!" it shrieked. "Oh, help me stop this infernal dancing!"

The demon stared as what had once been King Necrotus finally settled on the road, and promptly pranced sideways into the ditch. There was a thump and a flailing of limbs, then the deathly head rose into view, wobbling on its scrawny neck.

"Dear King," Bauchelain said, "you are free, and so I invite you to join us. We march into Quaint."

The corpse scrambled upright and stood wavering. "Good! Yes. I want that bastard's head! I want to rip it free and fling it into the air, then kick it down the street. Oh, let's visit my dear brother, yes, let's hurry!"

"It would seem," Bauchelain said as he led the others through the gateway, "that much of the present fabric of comportment has frayed in your city, King Necrotus, nay, torn asunder, and none of it through my doing. I am pleased to discover said evidence of my own cherished beliefs."

"What?" Storkul Purge demanded drunkenly, "are you talking 'bout?"

"Why, to transform the metaphor, that piety is but the thinnest patina, fashioned sufficiently opaque to disguise the true nature of our kind, yet brittle thin nonetheless."

"Who cares about all that?" Necrotus demanded. "I just want my throne back!"

"Ah, but will the citizens of your city accept the rule of an undead king?"

"They accept inbred brain-dead ones easily enough, sorceror," Necrotus said in a rasping growl, "so why not?"

"Well," Bauchelain said, "it is true enough that the common people delight in scandal when it comes to royalty. I suppose this could well qualify."

They paused in the street just inside the gate. The citizens were out tonight, both breathing and breathless, trim and vigorous and decrepit and disintegrating. Hoarse shouts and ragged, pealing screams, wild laughter and the shattering of empty bottles. Fires raging against the night sky, smoke tumbling and billowing. And, Ineb Cough saw, all manner of dramas being played out before their eyes.

A dead artist pursued a gallery owner, demanding money in a voice so whining and piteous that the demon felt compelled to kill the man a second time, not that it would do any good, but might well prove satisfying anyway. Even as Ineb considered setting off in pursuit, the two passed out of sight down a side street. Whilst from another a mob of mossy children—who'd clearly climbed out from some secret cemetery in someone's backyard—had found their murderer some time earlier and now marched into view, singing badly and waving about like trophies dismembered limbs. An odd detail that Ineb noted—the now torn apart murderer appeared to have been singular in having three arms, unless the children had grown careless, as children are wont to do, or perhaps did not know how to count very well. In any case, the urchins were happy and happy was good, wasn't it?

"This is sick," Storkul Purge said after a time. "I'm off to find my broth'l, where the sane people are."

Bauchelain bowed slightly in her direction. "Dear Well Knight, I thank you for your contribution to this night. I trust the wine has restored you?"

She blinked at him. "Restored? Oh yes. Restored, enlivened, invigoratedly enstored, lively, even." She then looked wildly about, meeting each set of eyes regarding her, fixing at last on the dead set. "Oh, you're not well, are you?"

The desiccated face twisted. "You just noticed?" Then Necrotus smiled. "Actually, I like that. You're my kind of woman . . . I think . . . now."

Storkul drew herself up. "Just so you don't make any wrong assumptions," she said haughtily, "I don't come cheap."

"Disgusting," Ineb Cough murmured, "but lovely."

"Shall we proceed?" Bauchelain asked Necrotus, who twitched in answer, then nodded.

Storkul Purge staggered off, presumably towards her old brothel.

King Necrotus made a brief, spasmodic effort to comb down his overlong, snarled and bird-dropping-gummed hair, then set out in a lilting half-step, feet kicking out. "Oh, I'm going to dance! All the way to the palace! Oh! How mortifying!"

The necromancer glanced over at Ineb Cough, brows lifting.

The demon nodded. "Absolutely. I'm with you two. Wouldn't miss it, no sir, not a chance."

"Actually," Bauchelain said, "I would you do something else for me."

"Is it sordid?"

"Why, yes, I suppose it is."

"All right, I'll do it."

IMID FACTALLO, THE BABY and Elas Sil came to within sight of the Grand Temple of the Lady's sprawling front entrance, and all three stared owlishly at the scores of bodies lying on the broad steps leading up to the dais and its altar.

"There's been a slaughter," Imid said in a quavering voice.

Elas grunted, then shook her head. "Not necessarily. See any blood? I don't see any blood."

"Well, it is rather dark—"

"No, even beneath those torch-stands."

"No-one's moving."

"I'll grant you that—it's damned odd, is what it is. Come on, Imid, let's get closer."

The two set out across the concourse. A tenement building two streets behind the temple was burning, showering sparks into the sky, making the Temple of the Lady a backlit silhouette that seemed sealed tight as a tomb, since no light was visible.

Snorting, Elas Sil said, "Typical. Drawn up as if under siege, which, I suppose, they are. Guess we won't be hearing any eerie proclamations from the altar any time in the near future, eh? The goddess is likely cowering in some hole."

"Shhh! By the Abyss, Elas, are you mad?"

"Mad? Yes, I am. Exceedingly mad."

They approached the steps and the scatter of bodies, bodies that then began to stir at the sound of their voices. Heads lifting, bleary eyes fixing upon them. Imid and Elas halted, fell silent.

"She won't save us!" one woman gasped. "Unhealthy people . . . everywhere! Drink . . . and smoke—everywhere! Ah, I feel sick. Just seeing them! Sick, nauseated, ill, unwell!"

"Sick, nauseated, ill, unwell!" a few others chanted.

Then they were all moaning the refrain. "*Sick, nauseated, ill, unwell!*"

"Lady below," Imid whispered, "Do-gooders! And look, they're withering before our eyes!"

"Remember our schooling as saints," Elas said. "Licentiousness, when all about, is a plague. A deathly, devouring host of demons, corrupting minds, bodies, souls. Licentiousness is the lurid escape from natural misery, when natural misery is the proper path to walk. Why? Because it is the only *honest* path."

Imid stared at her. "You didn't believe all that rubbish, did you?"

"Of course not, but these people do."

"And their convictions are killing them?"

"Precisely."

"But that's insane!" Baby mewling in his arms, Imid Factallo stepped forward. "Hear me! I am a Saint! Listen to me, all of you!"

The moaners fell silent, hopeful eyes gleaming in the firelight.

"Can't you see?" Imid demanded. "Sobriety means clear-eyed, and clear-eyed means you see the truth! You see just how unjust, cruel, indifferent and ugly your life really is! You see how other people are controlling you, every aspect of your miserable existence, and not just controlling you—they're screwing you over!"

Gasps and a single muted shriek answered Imid's careless curse.

"You can't say that!" "Foul, foul!" "No no no, I don't want to listen, no!"

The baby wailed.

"It's all lip-service!" Imid shouted. "Nobody in charge really gives a flying—"

"Silence!"

This last command was stentorian, ringing clear and loud from the temple's entrance. The do-gooders on the steps twisted round with cries of relief. Imid and Elas stared, as a grey-swathed nun marched up to stand to the right of the altar.

"It's the Stentorian Nun!" someone shouted.

The baby wailed again.

Imid's knees quivered as the grey woman stabbed an accusing finger at him. "You!" she hissed.

"Me!" Imid answered instinctively.

"Decrier of false truths!"

Elas Sil said, "What?"

"Blasphemer! Proclaimer of all that is Not to Be Known!"

"Well!" Imid shouted, suddenly, inexplicably emboldened, "too late for *that*, isn't it?"

More gasps. Worse, a crowd was gathering in the concourse behind them. Dead and living both.

"Oh," Elas said behind Imid, "you're in for it, now."

The nun lifted her arms out to the sides. "Adjudication is demanded!" she cried out. "The Lady of Beneficence shall speak! From her most Holy Altar, she shall speak!"

A strange, grinding noise came from the blockish stone beside the woman, then, a quavering voice, "Do I smell baby?"

ONE SLAP AGAINST THE massive, flabby cheek, then another, and another and another and—

"Stop! Please! Don't hurt me!"

"Nauseo? You awake?"

Bleary, sated eyes blinked up, the woeful expression dwindling away, to be replaced by a scowl. "Ineb Cough. What are you trying to do, kill me?"

"I was trying to wake you!"

"Was I asleep? Not surprising, you know. I'm filled to bursting—what a night! So unexpected!"

Ineb Cough was standing on the Demon of Corpulence's chest, or he thought he was—might have been just the left breast, since Nauseo Sloven had burgeoned to fill the entire alley, flesh piled up against either wall, more flesh sprawling and tumbled down to just short of the alley-mouth. "Even so," Ineb said, loosing a beery belch, "I need you up and around. We've a journey to make."

"A journey? Where?"

"Not far, I promise."

"I can't. It'll be too hard. I'm ready to explode—gods, where did all that greed come from?"

Ineb squatted down and scratched his pocked jaw. "All pent up, I suppose. Hiding, lurking. As for the food, well, seen any dogs in the streets? Cats? Horses? Me neither. The night's been a blood-bath, and it's not even half done. Who could have imagined all this?"

"What's happened, then?" Nauseo asked.

"Someone in the city's gone and hired two necromancers, Nauseo, to bring down this reign of terror." He pulled at his nose, which was itchy and runny with all the powder stuffed into it. "Seems they've made quite a start."

"Necromancers?"

"Yes. One of them's a conjurer and binder of demons, too, which makes me very nervous. Nervous, Nauseo, oh yes. Even so, he's yet to try for me, which I take as a good sign, weak as I was back then."

"No worries now, though, is there?" Nauseo shifted slightly and mounds of flesh rumbled and rolled beneath Ineb. "We're too strong, now. There's not a binder alive who could take us, emboldened as we now are."

"I expect you're right. So, it does seem as if these necromancers are staying true to their word. Pluck Macrotus from his throne, prop someone less horrible in his place, and Quaint returns to its normal, sane, decrepit state. Might even be Necrotus himself—the other one raised him, you know."

"Oh, joy!"

"Anyway, we've got to go. Have you seen Sloth lately?"

"Why, she was here earlier—"

From somewhere below, came a faint moan.

THOSE AMONG THE DENIZENS still capable of motion had moved on by the time Emancipor Reese spied Bauchelain, his master slowly walking with hands clasped behind his back, pausing every now and then for a word or two with various crippled dead and undead citizens, as he made his casual way towards the palace steps where sat the manservant.

Bauchelain peered up at Emancipor. "Is King Macrotus within?"

Emancipor nodded. "Oh yes, he's not going anywhere."

"I was in the company of King Necrotus," the necromancer said, looking round, "but it would seem we have become separated—there was a mob . . . well, the details aren't relevant. I take it, Mister Reese, that you have not been accosted by a corpse intent on entering the palace?"

"Afraid not, Master."

"Ah, I see. I am curious, has it struck you, Mister Reese, that events have quickened with a decidedly rapacious pace?"

"From the time that Invett Loath charged out of this building behind me, the whole city seems to have lost its mind."

"Invett Loath?"

"The Paladin of Purity, Master. Lord of the Well Knights. I am afraid . . . " Emancipor hesitated, "well, uh, I loaned him a kerchief. He'd bloodied his nose, you see. It was just common courtesy, how can I be blamed for that? I mean—"

"Mister Reese, please stop. I so dislike babbling. If I understand you, one of your many kerchiefs is now in the hands of this Paladin. And this is, in your mind, in some way significant."

"Master, do you recall that D'bayang field we passed through, oh, five, six days past?"

Bauchelain's eyes narrowed. "Go on, Mister Reese."

"Well, the buds were open, yes? They call 'em poppies but they aren't really poppies at all, as I am sure you know. Anyway, the air filled with spores—"

"Mister Reese, the air was not filled with spores, provided one remained on the road. As I recollect, however, there was some tumult, in your mind, at least, that resulted in you running madly through that field—with a kerchief covering your nose and mouth."

Emancipor's face reddened. "Korbal Broach asked me to carry that woman's lungs, the ones he took that morning—Master, they were still breathing!"

"A small favour, then—"

"Forgive me, Master, but it wasn't small in my eyes! Granted, it was unseemly, my horror and the ensuing panic. I admit it. But anyway. As you know, I so dislike enlivening alchemies—stupor and oblivion, yes, of course, at every opportunity. But enlivening, such as comes from D'bayang poppies? No. I despise that. Hence, the kerchief."

"Mister Reese, the kerchief you loaned the Paladin was not the one filled with D'bayang spores?"

"Alas, Master, it was. I'd meant to wash it, but—"

"The Paladin was afflicted?"

"I believe so. Of a sudden, zealousness overcame him."

"Possibly leading to . . . indiscriminate adjudication?"

"That's one way of putting it, aye."

Bauchelain stroked his beard. "Extraordinary. The guise of reasonableness, Mister Reese, permits all manner of intolerance and indeed, pernicious attack. Once that illusion is torn away, however, the terror of oppression becomes a random act, perhaps indeed an all-encompassing one." He paused, tapped one side of his nose with a long finger, then remorselessly continued, "That chest of coins rightly belongs to you, Mister Reese. Raising the dead? Entirely unnecessary, as it turns out. All that was required was a single, subtle push, at the hands of an innocent, somewhat naïve manservant."

Emancipor stared at the necromancer, desperate to refute the charge, to deny all culpability, yet unable to speak. In his mind, a risible refrain: *no, not me, no, no, it wasn't me. It was him. Who him? Anyone him! Just not me! No, not me, no, no . . . .*

"Mister Reese? You have lost all colour. Did I mention that I have not before seen your eyes so clear, the whites veritably startling? It is a force of nature that draws all things down to the earth. I therefore imagine the flow of a multitude of toxins now swelling your poor feet. They must, I fear, be bled. Thoroughly. Of course, now is not the time—no, make no entreaties otherwise, Mister Reese. Now, if you please, lead me to King Macrotus."

Emancipor frowned, then blinked. Feet? Bleeding? Macrotus? "I am happy to lead you to Macrotus, Master, and you may speak to him all you like, I am sure, although I suspect it won't do much good."

"I rarely speak in order to do good, Mister Reese. Now, shall we be on our way?"

INVETT LOATH HAD NEVER felt more alive, so alive it was killing him, but that was fine since it seemed he was doing a fair share of killing himself, if the blood smeared on his sword was any indication, and he was reasonably certain that it was indeed fairly indicative that he had been practicing holy adjudication upon the unwholesome unwashed cretins who dared consider themselves worthy citizens of Quaint, adjudication that was only proper, as was his right, nay his obligation as the Paladin of Purity, the Paladin of Perfection, leading the vanguard of vigor to their healthy, thankful deaths, and if he and his blessed vanguard trod on a few babies, toddlers and weak-boned old folk along the way, well, there was nothing to be done for that, was there, not when the cause was just, so just it blinded like the sun's own fire, all-consuming, scouraging the meat from the bones and yes, he was sure scouraging was a proper word and why shouldn't it be, was he not the Paladin of Proper, he most certainly was and look! the night's still young, exceedingly bright, in fact, given all those burning hovels and their burning denizens, none of whom deserved a less sordid, less scorching death because adjudication came in all forms, in all sizes including ratty blankets swaddling shrieking undeniably irritating whelps all laid out plump and yummy by the nuns who might well be pretty behind those veils who could tell not that such thoughts were acceptable, they being nuns and all, and he the Paladin of Probity marching down this street of flame was there not some cavern in the underworld that was nothing but fire and torment, maybe not but there should be, as far as Invett Loath was concerned, some preserved place of eternal pain just for all those unhealthy turds badly clothed in human skin, the fires could crinkle it back, rupturing the meat beneath, and how they would writhe and spit and heave up vile fluids in an endless torrent of foul toxins and all the flesh would tumble out, fold upon fold, gelatinous and pocked with big, suppurating pores, the flesh filling the street and how was he to get past this? By the Lady, it lived!

"Oomph!" the massive body gusted at the sudden impact.

Invett Loath's wild charge was brought short. He plunged into flabby folds, then popped back out to land on his backside, blinking water from his eyes, fresh blood streaming down from his swollen nose.

"That hurt!" a piping squeal.

The Paladin leapt to his feet, cloth at his face. He could get around this! He had a sword. Cut, cut and dice and chop and cleave and hack in twain! With a roar, Invett Loath raised his blade high.

Twenty-odd paces away, the barrel-sized, misshapen blob that was Nauseo Sloven's sweaty face, spread out to the sides and above and below in a expression of terror, the tiny eyes widening and bulging sufficient to push away the puffy flesh, and the demon screamed.

And flinched back, narrowly avoiding the descending sword.

Iron rang on cobbles.

Panicked, Nauseo Sloven lunged forward, heaving his mass to grapple with the Paladin before he could swing again. Stretched, oily skin slimed over Invett Loath in a desperate embrace. Pores sprouting curly hairs, the flesh around them enflamed and raised up like tiny volcanoes, pressed indiscriminately against the struggling Paladin, squirting volcanically foul juices.

Nauseo's arm drew inward once again, dragging the squirming figure into his right armpit.

Where all manner of horrors resided.

Invett Loath could not breathe. But he didn't need to breathe! He was the Paladin of—of—he was asphyxiating! Swallowed in fleshy darkness, matted hairs like worms sliding across his face, pimples bursting, a crevasse of skin spreading to smear years-old greasy dirt across his lips—oh, the taste, what was it? What did it remind him of? Yoghurt?

Yoghurt. Invett Loath's last conscious word, sobbing dreadful in his mind.

"GIVE ME *that baby!*"

Imid Factallo flinched back at that reptilian hiss. In his arms, the babe fell silent, eyes suddenly wide as it stared up at the saint.

"Give it to me!"

Imid looked across at the Stentorian Nun. Their public debate had collapsed into a ruin of vicious insults which, while entertaining to the crowd, were otherwise worthless. One rather strange consequence of the exchange was that the nun's clothing had become disheveled. Even her veil had begun to sag at one corner, revealing half of the hate-twisted mouth.

In which Imid now saw pointy teeth. He stabbed out an accusatory finger. "She's got filed teeth! She wants my baby! *She's a cannibal!*"

Mobs were unpredictable beasts, particularly after a night of unspeakable trauma. Among this one could be found mothers who had lost their young ones to the Temple, to nuns just like this one. With her hungry snarl and shark-like teeth. The shouted proclamation from Imid Factallo required a moment of stunned silence in which to do its work, time sufficient for various terrible details to fall in line.

Then—screams, a surge of vengeful humanity, grasping hands, ugly animal sounds.

The nun bleated and made to flee.

She did not get far.

A horrifying scene ensued, Imid Factallo's witnessing thereof cut short when Elas Sil used both hands to pull him away, round to the other side of the altar, then stumbling onward towards the temple doors. Seeing their destination, Imid pulled back. "No! Not in there!"

"You idiot!" Elas Sil hissed. "Those teeth weren't filed! They were rotten! Just stumps! That woman *slurps* her meals, Imid! Understand me?"

He looked back, and saw very little left of the Stentorian Nun. "I could have sworn they were pointed—"

"They weren't!"

"Then . . . baby soup!"

"Oh now, really!" They approached the doors, and Elas Sil added, "Mind you, what a great way to close a debate. I'll have to remember that one."

"They looked pretty pointy to me," Imid persisted in a grumble.

Elas Sil grasped the iron ring and tugged.

To their surprise the door swung open. They peered into the gloom. An empty chamber, longer than it was wide, the ceiling arched and sheathed in gold leaf, and no-one about.

"Where is everyone?" Imid wondered in a whisper.

"Let's find out," Elas Sil said.

They crept into the Grand Temple.

KING NECROTUS THE NIHILE was feeling decidedly unwell. For one, his left arm had fallen off. And he'd found bats nesting in his crotch. They'd fled, thankfully, some time during his frenetic dancing on the wall. Even so, the little claws from which they had hung were sharp, and now that brittle sensation raced through his withered flesh, sensation so painfully reawakened, he found certain parts aching abominably.

Stumbling over his own arm was an unexpected development. One moment swinging amiably at his side, the next fouling his feet, resulting in a face-flat fall that broke something in his jaw, where things now rattled loose whenever he turned his head. All of this in consequence to his panicked flight from that mob, a mob that had been perniciously hunting down the dead and tearing them apart. Base prejudices hid beneath even the most placid of surfaces, which came as little surprise to the king known as the Nihile, but had proved inconvenient nonetheless.

And now he was lost. In his own city. Hopelessly lost.

There were no burning buildings nearby, and so he stumbled along in darkness, right arm tucked under his left (the Royal Seamstress could do wonders, assuming she still lived), in search of a familiar landmark.

Unexpected, therefore, the strange transformation of the street he walked down, the sudden swirling of mists, the leaden smear of sky, and the massive arched gate appearing at the far end, a gate composed entirely of bones, from which a hunched, scrawny figure hobbled into view.

Necrotus halted twenty paces from the figure, who also stopped, leaning heavily on a gnarled cane. The figure then lifted a skeletal hand, and beckoned.

Overwhelming compulsion tugged at Necrotus and he found himself slowly drawn forward. "Who are you?" he hissed.

Hooded head cocked to one side. "The Lord of Death? Harvester of Souls? The Bony Fisherman who casts his all-encompassing net?" A sigh. "No, just one of his minions. Have I not great potential? I keep saying so, but does he ever listen? No, never. I keep the path swept clean, don't I? Polish the skulls of the Gate, yes? Look at them—blinding, even the teeth are entirely devoid of tartar! I am no slouch, no sir, not in the least!"

Necrotus struggled to escape, yet watched, in horror, as his feet were dragged forward, one then the other, again and again, closer to that dread gate. "No! I've been raised! You can't have me!"

The minion grunted. "Korbal Broach. One abominable act after another, oh we despise him, yes we do. Despise and more, for I am tasked to pursue him. To capture him. That must mean something! Great potential, and so I must prove my worth. I have gathered a legion—all of Korbal Broach's victims—and we will find him, oh yes, find him!"

"Go away!" Necrotus cried.

The minion started. "What?"

"Go away! I hate you! I'm not going through that infernal gate!"

In a small voice, "You . . . *hate* me?"

"Yes!"

"But what have I ever done to you?"

"You're compelling me to walk through that gate!"

"Don't blame me about that! I am only doing my job. It's nothing personal—"

"Of course it's personal, you scrawny idiot!"

"Oh, you're all the same! I drag you out of your miserable existence, and are you ever grateful? No, not once! You and your precious beliefs, your host of conceits and pointless faiths! Your elaborate self-delusions seeking to cheat the inevitable. And you hate me? No, I hate you! All of you!" With that the minion spun round and hobbled stiffly back through the gate.

There was a loud slam and the scene in front of Necrotus dissolved, revealing the slightly more familiar street of Quaint he had been stumbling down earlier. He stared about, bewildered. "He...he didn't want me!" Well, that was good, wasn't it? Then why did he feel so...offended?

King Necrotus the Nihile resumed walking. He still needed to find out precisely where he was.

A double thump at his feet. He halted and stared down. Two arms were lying on the cobbles. "Shit."

Then his head rolled off, left temple crunching hard on the stones, his vision tumbling wildly.

Oh, this was not going well at all.

*B*AUCHELAIN HAD CLIMBED into the apparatus, deftly ducking rocking levers and edging round ratcheting gears until he was next to King Macrotus.

Standing near the spilled supper left on the floor by the servant, Emancipor Reese watched with reluctant admiration. The necromancer was not one for exercise, yet remained lean and lithe, ever in fighting form on those rare occasions when sorcery, guile, deceit and back-stabbing failed. Physically, he looked to be about sixty, albeit a fit sixty, yet he moved with a dancer's grace. The result of good living? Possibly. More likely alchemy.

"Well, Master?" the manservant called. "How many days, do you think?"

Bauchelain leaned forward for a closer examination. "At least two weeks," he said. "I believe his heart burst. Sudden and indeed catastrophic." The necromancer glanced back. "How did you know?"

Emancipor shrugged. "He wasn't eating."

Bauchelain made his way back. "Proponents of vigorous exercise are mostly unaware," the sorceror said, "that exercise as a notion, discrete from labour, is a gift of civilisation, derived from tiered social status and the leisure time thus afforded. True laborers care nothing for exercise, naturally." He stepped cleared of the clanking, wheezing apparatus, paused to brush dust from his cloak. "Accordingly, one salient fact that laborers well know, but appears to be lost on those who fanatically exercise, is that the body, its organs, its muscles and its bones, will inevitably wear out. I believe, Mister Reese, that, for example, there are a set number of beats of which a heart is capable. In similar manner all muscles and bones and other organs are allotted a specific limit to their functioning." He gestured grandly back at the laboring corpse of King Macrotus the Overwhelmingly Considerate. "To hasten one's own body to those limits is, to my mind, the highest folly."

Emancipor grunted. "Master, I really need to get out of this city."

"Ah, that would be withdrawal."

They stared at each for a moment.

Then Bauchelain cleared his throat. "One last task awaits me. Given the unexpected turn of events this night, Mister Reese, I believe your tasks within Quaint are done. Thus, I grant you leave to, uh, leave."

"I can't thank you enough, Master."

"No matter. One final thing. Can you give me directions to the Grand Temple of the Lady of Beneficence?"

"Of course, Master."

ARM IN ARM WITH revelers and in the midst of a bawdy, drunken crowd, the Demon of Vice staggered into the vast, seething mob filling the concourse fronting the Grand Temple. He was singing, at the top of his voice, a song he had never heard before. Life was wonderful, again, and this was a night Ineb Cough would not forget in a long while. Or not remember at all. It didn't matter which.

They stumbled over pieces of corpses, many of them still eager to party, if the twitching and writhing of dismembered limbs was any indication. A number of tenement fires had leapt closer to the temple, bathing it in lurid light. Near the steps was the mass of putrescent but doggedly throbbing flesh that was the Demon of Corpulence. He was surrounded by impromptu feasting, huge slabs of undercooked, dripping meat making the rounds, greasy smeared faces splashed with the light of rapture, and people were being sick everywhere, unaccustomed as they—well, no, Ineb corrected himself—they were sick with excess, glorious excess.

He saw Sloth being carried in atop a score of hands. Seeing Ineb Cough, she managed a faint white-gloved wave.

So, all were gathered, and need only await their brilliant saviour, Bauchelain, on his way to pronounce upon the city its fate. Ineb was delirious with anticipation.

"SWEETIES, I'M HERE!" Storkul Purge spread her arms out to her sides and held the gesture. Before her, in the Orgy Room on the top floor of Hurla's Brothel, shapes moved about in the gloom. Lots of shapes, she realised, all seemingly on their hands and knees. A good sign. In fact, judging from the grunting and squeaking, lots of good signs.

Except, of course, for the smell.

One figure rose up hesitantly before her.

Tragically, her eyes had begun to adjust to the darkness. "What is all that smeared on you?" she demanded.

A wavering voice, "Keeps them happy, you see."

"Who?"

"Why," the little man gestured behind him, "my pigs, of course."

Pigs? By the Abyss, they *were* pigs! "But this is a brothel! Worst, this is the third floor! What are all these disgusting animals doing here when I wanted the *normal* disgusting animals!"

"I'm hiding them, of course! Everyone has gone mad! They want to slaughter all my beauties, but I won't let them! Who'd look on the top floor of a brothel? Why, no-one! No-one but you, and you're not here to lead my pigs to slaughter...are you?"

She considered for a long moment, then slowly lowered her arms, and sighed. "Fine, I'll just hold my breath. Get undressed, old man, this one's on the house."

"I—I can't do that! They'll get jealous!"

Too much pent-up frustration by far. Storkul Purge screamed.

WANDERING BEMUSED in the subterranean chambers and corridors beneath the temple, Imid Factallo, his baby and Elas Sil could all hear the roaring from somewhere overhead. Ominous, as if a terrible slaughter was taking place in the city's streets. Or so they believed, since their last sight of the above world had been the horrid death of the Stentorian Nun.

Yet here, below, there was naught but silence. Where were the nuns? The confiscated children? They had found no-one, no-one at all.

"Shh!" Elas Sil's hand clutched his arm.

"I didn't say anything!"

"Shhh!"

Now, close by, a gentle murmuring of voices. They were standing in a corridor. Before them was a T-intersection, with a door directly opposite them. Faint lantern light leaked from its seams, musty with scented oils.

Elas pulled him along, up to the door.

"This is it," Imid whispered.

She looked across at him.

"Where they prepare the babies," Imid explained, his heart thudding hard in his chest. He licked his lips, his mouth suddenly terribly dry. "They lead them in by the hand, the smiling nuns. Then *whack*! Down comes the cleaver! Chop chop, bones into the cauldron, some old hag stirring with a huge iron ladle, spittle hanging from her toothless mouth. All those tiny voices, silenced forever!" He stared down at the slumbering child in his arms. "We've come to the wrong place, Elas!"

"You've gone mad! You sound like . . . like a *parent!*"

And she flung open the door.

Light spilled over them.

A sea of faces. Cherubic faces, countless children of all ages.

All of whom cried out, "Inside, quick! Oh, shut the door!" More of a cacophony of voices, truth be told, but both Imid and Elas comprehended those two commands at the very least.

They stumbled into the domed chamber.

And the door was slammed shut behind them.

Children rushed forward upon seeing the swaddled baby. "Ooh! Another one! He? She? Is it well? Not sick yet, oh blessed Lady, not yet sick!"

Imid recoiled slightly at the upward grasping hands. "Get away, you horrid creatures! Sick? No-one's sick! No-one, I tell you!"

"What," Elas Sil demanded, "are you all doing here?"

"We are being well!"

"Well what?"

A slightly older girl stepped forward. "We're being protected. From the outer world, that horrible, dirty, sickly place!"

"Sickly?" Elas repeated bemusedly. "What do you mean?"

"There are foul things out there—things that will make us sick. Animals, to make us sick! Flies, birds, bats, mice, rats, all diseased and waiting to make us sick! And people! Coughing, sniveling, wiping themselves everywhere! There are wayward fumes, emanating from anuses and worse. And wagons that might run us over, stairs we might fall down, walls we might walk into. You must join us, here, where it's safe!"

"And healthy," another piped up.

"What's it like?" a third child asked.

Elas Sil blinked. "What is what like?"

"The world?"

"Stop that, Chimly!" the first girl scolded. "You know that curiosity is deadly!"

Someone in the crowd coughed.

Everyone swung round, and the first girl hissed, "*Who did that?*"

"Now!" Imid shouted. And, thankfully, Elas Sil understood. In unison they turned and scrabbled at the door latch.

Behind them: "Look! They're getting away!"

Then the door was open, and the two saints with their charge fled out into the corridor.

"Get them!"

They ran.

K ING NECROTUS THE NIHILE was seeing things from a new angle. Sideways, slightly upside-down. He had tried locomotion by wiggling his ears, but the effect had been meager. Clearly, his facial and scalp muscles weren't designed to aid in the physical transportation of his head. That's what the body normally attached to it did. It had been a pathetic conceit.

A large polished boot stepped into his view.

"Hello?" Necrotus called up.

The boot shifted, then the heel drew upwards and a hand settled on the king's head, tilting it to one side. Necrotus found himself looking up at a crouching Bauchelain.

"Abyss averted!" the king sighed in relief. "I am so glad you found me. Can you see my body? It's the one without any arms— and no head, naturally. It can't have gone far... can it?"

Bauchelain collected Necrotus in both hands and straightened. There was something oddly disturbing about the necromancer's expression as he studied the king.

"Am I speaking only in my head?" Necrotus asked. "Uh, as it were. I mean, can you hear me?"

"I can hear you fine, King Necrotus," Bauchelain replied after a moment, angling the head this way and that.

"Just a little off the top?" the king asked in a half-snarl.

"I have," Bauchelain said, " a glass case that would fit you nicely."

"You wouldn't!"

"Yes, a nice fit indeed. Well, this is a bonus, isn't it?"

"That's diabolical!"

"Why yes, thank you."

Necrotus was tucked under Bauchelain's left arm, affording him a jostling view of the street they now walked down. The king was furious, but there was little he could do about it. Oh, his kingdom for a body! "You'll keep it wiped clean, won't you?"

"Of course, King Necrotus," Bauchelain replied. "Ah, I see the edges of a crowd. I believe we approach the Grand Temple."

"And what are we going to do there?"

"Why, a grand unveiling to close this fell night."

"IT'S A TUNNEL OF SORTS," Imid Factallo said.

"I can see that," Elas Sil snapped.

"We've no choice. I can hear those terrifying little whelps."

"I know I know! All right, I'll lead, and close that panel behind us."

They had stumbled on the secret passage only because someone had left the small door wide open. From somewhere up the corridor behind them came the dread, blood-curdling sounds of excited children.

Imid followed Elas into the tunnel's narrow confines, then twisted about to tug the panel back in place. Sudden darkness.

"By the Lady's never-sucked teats!"

"Elas Sil!"

"Oh shut up! I'm a woman, I can curse about things like that. Wait, it's not as dark up ahead. Come on, and hasn't that baby of yours been asleep a long time? You sure it's not dead?"

"Well, it peed on me halfway down that last corridor, and last I looked it was smiling."

"Huh. It ever amazes me women get talked into motherhood."

"Talked into it? Don't be ridiculous, Elas. They're desperate for it!"

"Only once and that once is the first time."

"I don't believe you."

"I don't care what you believe. You're a man, after all. All I know is, I happen to value a full night's sleep a lot more than flinging another urchin into this all-too-crowded city, then sagging everywhere as my only reward. No thanks. I intend to stay pert forever."

"I'm pretty sure it doesn't work that way," Imid said.

"You've only your mother for comparison and she had you, didn't she?"

"So how come you don't get pregnant—I mean, what we did this afternoon—"

"Willpower. Look, it's getting lighter—there's some kind of room up ahead."

"Hear all that noise above us? Something awful's happening in the concourse, Elas Sil—and it seems we're getting closer to it, or maybe it's getting closer to us."

"Abyss below, Imid, do you ever stop moaning?"

They clambered out into a strange circular room, the floor set with pavestones except in the middle, where rested a single slab of polished wood that shifted beneath them, as if unanchored. The domed ceiling was barely high enough for them to kneel anywhere but in the middle, and it turned out the extra room in the centre came from a square shaft leading straight up, as far as they could see. Off to one side sat a lantern, burning out the last of its oil. The room smelled of sweat.

"Now what?" Imid asked.

"Put that damned baby down," Elas Sil said, oddly breathless.

Imid adjusted the blanket's folds, then gently laid the baby to one side, onto the pavestones. It cooed, then rolled onto its side and spat up. Briefly. Once done, it settled onto its back once more, closed its eyes and was asleep. Imid backed away.

The lantern dimmed, then winked out.

Hot skin—arms, thighs—"Elas!" Imid gasped as he was pulled round. "Not in front of the baby!"

But she wasn't listening.

THE NECROMANCER HAD THAT certain quality, Ineb Cough reflected, to clear a path before him, seemingly effortless and without a word spoken. Sounds died away, as if Bauchelain was a pebble of silence flung into a loud pond. A pond filled with loud fish, that is. Perhaps. In any case, Ineb marveled at the way things got quiet as Bauchelain, an extra head tucked under one arm, made his way to the temple steps and ascended to the platform, positioning himself to the left of the altar as he faced the now rapt crowd.

The necromancer cocked his head (his own, the one atop his shoulders) for a moment, and Ineb Cough felt a subtle outflow of sorcerous power—power of such terrible magnitude that the Demon felt his knees weaken beneath him. For all his confidence, and Nauseo Sloven's, it was now clear that Ineb, Corpulence and Sloth were as babes before this man. "He could take us," the Demon of Vice whimpered, a bottle of wine falling from his hand to crash on the cobbles. "He could bind us and not raise a single bead of sweat in the effort. Oh. Oh no."

Bauchelain raised his right hand and a sudden hush descended upon the massed citizens in the concourse. Under his left arm, King Necrotus's head faced outward as well, bizarre grimacing expressions writhing on its withered features. The necromancer spoke, "People of Quaint, hear me! You have, until this night, been the victims of a terrible deceit. Said deceit will be revealed to you here, and now." That upraised hand then slowly closed into a fist.

A muted scream from ... somewhere, and nowhere.

A figure blurred into being directly beneath Bauchelain's hand.

Ineb Cough started. "That!" he shouted. "That's Lust! The Demoness of Lust! That's Agin Again!"

The voluptuous, naked woman, bound in place by Bauchelain's conjuring, shrieked in terror.

"An imposter!" the necromancer bellowed. "Hiding in the guise of the Lady of Beneficence! Do you think Lust thrives only in matters of sex and sordid indulgences? If so, my friends, you are wrong! Lust is born of obsession! Obsession begets zealotry! Zealotry breeds deadly intolerance! Intolerance leads to oppression, and oppression to tyranny. And tyranny, citizens of Quaint, leads to—"

"The end of civilisation!" a thousand voices roared.

Lust cried, "I'm sorry! I'm sorry! I didn't mean it!"

"Indeed," Bauchelain said in response to the crowd's proclamation, ignoring Agin Again, who now wept unconvincingly. "And so," the necromancer continued, "wisdom returns to Quaint. Your faith had been subverted, twisted into hateful fanaticism. But of that, no more need be said. It does grieve me, alas, to inform you now of the death of King Macrotus." He shook his head. "No, not by my hand. He is dead of exercise. And has been for some time. Alas, he could not be here to tell you himself, for the chamber where his body resides is warded, and so he cannot be raised. But it would do you all well to pay a visit to his Royal chamber. Consider it a worthy shrine to ever remind you of the deadly lure of lustful activity left unrestrained."

He paused then, looking about, studying the upturned faces, then nodded as if to himself. "Citizens, I shall now proclaim your new rulers. Worthy individuals indeed, iconic representations of all that is proper, individuals you will be delighted to emulate in all matters of behaviour and comportment." Another gesture, and Agin Again was suddenly released. Wailing, she leapt upright, then fled.

From the altar came a heavy grinding sound.

Bauchelain half-turned, twitched a finger and the altar rose into the air.

In time to reveal, rising from a subterranean platform, Quaint's new king and queen.

Locked into a most amorous embrace and momentarily oblivious to their own arrival, so intent was their missionary zeal.

A draft such as is common during the night alerted them to the change of venue. And two heads lifted clear, looked out dumbly upon the vast crowd.

Who stared back in shocked silence.

Then went wild.

*T*HE SUN WAS CLEAR of the horizon by the time Bauchelain returned to the wagon and the camp on the hill outside the smoke-wreathed city.

Emancipor watched him from a low to the ground, sideways perspective, lying as he was on his back with his bared feet propped high against the side of a wagon wheel.

The necromancer was carrying a head under one arm, and he strode up to the manservant. "Dear Mister Reese, may I ask, what are you doing?"

"It's the toxins, Master. I'm draining my feet. No need for bleeding, no, no need at all."

"I can see by the murky cast of your eyes," Bauchelain said, "that such medical intervention would be pointless in any case."

"True enough," Emancipor replied.

Bauchelain strode to the back of the wagon, and Emancipor heard him rummaging about for a time. After a moment, he reappeared with a glass case that Emancipor had never seen before. "Now, Mister Reese, assuming your feet are now cleansed, as best as they can be, might I suggest you prepare to break our fast?"

Emancipor lowered his legs and struggled upright. "Gods below," he swore, "my legs have gone numb." Even so, he managed to hobble over towards the hearth, which was still smouldering. "I have mulled wine, Master. Shall I pour you a cup?"

"Hmm? Yes, excellent idea. And for yourself as well."

"Thank you, Master." Emancipor paused to light his pipe. "Ah, much better," he said, blowing smoke. Cut short by a hacking cough, forcing him to launch a slimy ball of stuff into the fire, where it flared into strangely hued flames for a moment before sizzling in the more expected manner. Emancipor stuck the pipe back between his teeth and puffed merrily as he poured the wine.

A flutter of wings nearby announced the arrival of Korbal Broach. The crow hopped over to watch as Bauchelain set King Necrotus's head inside the glass case, then placed the container on the buckboard. The king looked to be talking, but no sound issued forth, for which Emancipor was thankful.

The manservant rose and handed Bauchelain a cup. "A toast, Master?"

"A toast? Well, why not? Please, proceed, Mister Reese."

Emancipor raised his cup. "The Healthy Dead!"

Bauchelain almost smiled. Almost, but not quite, which was about as much as Emancipor had expected. "Indeed," the necromancer said, raising his own cup, "The Healthy Dead."

In the glass case, King Necrotus smiled broadly, as the dead are wont to do.